P9-CJC-138

DATE DUE

MR 1 '99		
ME 8 05		
AP 9		
JE 9 10		

NO LONGER AT EASE

BY CHINUA ACHEBE

FAWCETT PREMIER • NEW YORK

A Fawcett Premier Book
Published by Ballantine Books
Copyright © 1960 by Chinua Achebe

The author and publishers gratefully acknowledge permission from Messrs Faber and Faber Ltd to reproduce the quotation on page 6.

Cover Art by Leo and Diane Dillon

ISBN 0-449-30023-4

This edition published by arrangement with
Astor-Honor, Inc.

Manufactured in the United States of America

First Fawcett Premier Edition: October 1969
First Ballantine Books Edition: January 1984
Twenty-fourth Printing: May 1991

For Christie

We returned to our places, these Kingdoms,
But no longer at ease here, in the old dispensation,
With an alien people clutching their gods.
I should be glad of another death.

    T. S. ELIOT, "The Journey of the Magi"

NO LONGER AT EASE

A NOTE ABOUT THE TITLE

The title for Chinua Achebe's first novel, *Things Fall Apart*, is taken from William Butler Yeats' poem, "The Second Coming," and the title for his second novel, *No Longer at Ease*, from T. S. Eliot's "The Journey of the Magi." As Judith Gleason points out in *This Africa*, the choice of titles reflects the author's awareness of a debilitation that Okonkwo foresees in *Things Fall Apart*: "For *Things Fall Apart* comes from the world of Yeats' cataclysmic vision, and how the Irish poet would have appreciated the wild old Nigerian! *No Longer at Ease* comes from the anticlimactic world to which Eliot's magi return. The career of the grandson Okonkwo [the hero of *No Longer at Ease*, grandson of the hero of *Things Fall Apart*] ends not with a matchet's swing but with a gavel's tap."

CHAPTER ONE

FOR THREE OR FOUR WEEKS OBI OKONKWO HAD BEEN
steeling himself against this moment. And when he walked
into the dock that morning he thought he was fully
prepared. He wore a smart palm-beach suit and appeared
unruffled and indifferent. The proceeding seemed to be of
little interest to him. Except for one brief moment at the
very beginning when one of the counsel had got into
trouble with the judge.

"This court begins at nine o'clock. Why are you late?"

Whenever Mr. Justice William Galloway, Judge of the
High Court of Lagos and the Southern Cameroons,
looked at a victim he fixed him with his gaze as a collector
fixes his insect with formalin. He lowered his head like a
charging ram and looked over his gold-rimmed spectacles
at the lawyer.

"I am sorry, Your Honor," the man stammered. "My
car broke down on the way."

The judge continued to look at him for a long time.
Then he said very abruptly:

"All right, Mr. Adeyemi. I accept your excuse. But I
must say I'm getting sick and tired of these constant
excuses about the problem of locomotion."

There was suppressed laughter at the bar. Obi Okonkwo
smiled a wan and ashy smile and lost interest again.

Every available space in the courtroom was taken up.

There were almost as many people standing as sitting. The case had been the talk of Lagos for a number of weeks and on this last day anyone who could possibly leave his job was there to hear the judgment. Some civil servants paid as much as ten shillings and sixpence to obtain a doctor's certificate of illness for the day.

Obi's listlessness did not show any signs of decreasing even when the judge began to sum up. It was only when he said: "I cannot comprehend how a young man of your education and brilliant promise could have done this" that a sudden and marked change occurred. Treacherous tears came into Obi's eyes. He brought out a white handkerchief and rubbed his face. But he did it as people do when they wipe sweat. He even tried to smile and belie the tears. A smile would have been quite logical. All that stuff about education and promise and betrayal had not taken him unawares. He had expected it and rehearsed this very scene a hundred times until it had become as familiar as a friend.

In fact, some weeks ago when the trial first began, Mr. Green, his boss, who was one of the Crown witnesses, had also said something about a young man of great promise. And Obi had remained completely unmoved. Mercifully he had recently lost his mother, and Clara had gone out of his life. The two events following closely on each other had dulled his sensibility and left him a different man, able to look words like *education* and *promise* squarely in the face. But now when the supreme moment came he was betrayed by treacherous tears.

Mr. Green had been playing tennis since five o'clock. It was most unusual. As a rule his work took up so much of his time that he rarely played. His normal exercise was a short walk in the evenings. But today he had played with a friend who worked for the British Council. After the game they retired to the club bar. Mr. Green had a light-yellow sweater over his white shirt, and a white towel hung from his neck. There were many other Europeans in the bar, some half-sitting on the high stools and some standing in groups of twos and threes drinking cold beer, orange squash or gin and tonic.

"I cannot understand why he did it," said the British Council man thoughtfully. He was drawing lines of water with his finger on the back of his mist-covered glass of ice-cold beer.

"I can," said Mr. Green simply. "What I can't understand is why people like you refuse to face facts." Mr. Green was famous for speaking his mind. He wiped his red face with the white towel on his neck. "The African is corrupt through and through." The British Council man looked about him furtively, more from instinct than necessity, for although the club was now open to them technically, few Africans went to it. On this particular occasion there was none, except of course the stewards who served unobtrusively. It was quite possible to go in, drink, sign a check, talk to friends and leave again without noticing these stewards in their white uniforms. If everything went right you did not see them.

"They are all corrupt," repeated Mr. Green. "I'm all for equality and all that. I for one would hate to live in South Africa. But equality won't alter facts."

"What facts?" asked the British Council man, who was relatively new to the country. There was a lull in the general conversation, as many people were now listening to Mr. Green without appearing to do so.

"The fact that over countless centuries the African has been the victim of the worst climate in the world and of every imaginable disease. Hardly his fault. But he has been sapped mentally and physically. We have brought him Western education. But what use is it to him? He is . . ." He was interrupted by the arrival of another friend.

"Hello, Peter. Hello, Bill."

"Hello."

"Hello."

"May I join you?"

"Certainly."

"Most certainly. What are you drinking? Beer? Right. Steward. One beer for this master."

"What kind, sir?"

"Heineken."

"Yes, sir."

"We were talking about this young man who took a bribe."

"Oh, yes."

Somewhere on the Lagos mainland the Umuofia Progressive Union was holding an emergency meeting. Umuofia is an Ibo village in Eastern Nigeria and the home town of Obi Okonkwo. It is not a particularly big village, but its inhabitants call it a town. They are very proud of its past when it was the terror of their neighbors, before the white man came and leveled everybody down. Those Umuofians (that is the name they call themselves) who leave their home town to find work in towns all over Nigeria regard themselves as sojourners. They return to Umuofia every two years or so to spend their leave. When they have saved up enough money they ask their relations at home to find them a wife, or they build a "zinc" house on their family land. No matter where they are in Nigeria, they start a local branch of the Umuofia Progressive Union.

In recent weeks the Union had met several times over Obi Okonkwo's case. At the first meeting, a handful of people had expressed the view that there was no reason why the Union should worry itself over the troubles of a prodigal son who had shown great disrespect to it only a little while ago.

"We paid eight hundred pounds to train him in England," said one of them. "But instead of being grateful he insults us because of a useless girl. And now we are being called together again to find more money for him. What does he do with his big salary? My own opinion is that we have already done too much for him."

This view, although accepted as largely true, was not taken very seriously. For, as the President pointed out, a kinsman in trouble had to be saved, not blamed; anger against a brother was felt in the flesh, not in the bone. And so the Union decided to pay for the services of a lawyer from their funds.

But this morning the case was lost. That was why another emergency meeting had been convened. Many people had already arrived at the house of the President on Moloney Street, and were talking excitedly about the judgment.

"I knew it was a bad case," said the man who had opposed the Union's intervention from the start. "We are just throwing money away. What do our people say? He that fights for a ne'er-do-well has nothing to show for it except a head covered in earth and grime."

But this man had no following. The men of Umuofia were prepared to fight to the last. They had no illusions about Obi. He was, without doubt, a very foolish and self-willed young man. But this was not the time to go into that. The fox must be chased away first; after that the hen might be warned against wandering into the bush.

When the time for warning came the men of Umuofia could be trusted to give it in full measure, pressed down and flowing over. The President said it was a thing of shame for a man in the senior service to go to prison for twenty pounds. He repeated twenty pounds, spitting it out. "I am against people reaping where they have not sown. But we have a saying that if you want to eat a toad you should look for a fat and juicy one."

"It is all lack of experience," said another man. "He should not have accepted the money himself. What others do is tell you to go and hand it to their houseboy. Obi tried to do what everyone does without finding out how it was done." He told the proverb of the house rat who went swimming with his friend the lizard and died from cold, for while the lizard's scales kept him dry the rat's hairy body remained wet.

The President, in due course, looked at his pocket watch and announced that it was time to declare the meeting open. Everybody stood up and he said a short prayer. Then he presented three kola nuts to the meeting. The oldest man present broke one of them, saying another kind of prayer while he did it. "He that brings kola nuts brings life," he said. "We do not seek to hurt any man, but if any man seeks to hurt us may he break his neck." The congregation answered *Amen*. "We are strangers in this land. If good comes to it may we have our share." *Amen*. "But if bad comes let it go to the owners of the land who know what gods should be appeased." *Amen*. "Many towns have four or five or even ten of their sons in European posts in this city. Umuofia has only one. And now our enemies say that even that one is too many for us. But our ancestors will not agree to such a thing." *Amen*. "An only palm fruit does not get lost in the fire." *Amen*.

Obi Okonkwo was indeed an only palm-fruit. His full name was Obiajulu—"the mind at last is at rest"; the mind being his father's of course, who, his wife having borne him four daughters before Obi, was naturally becoming a little anxious. Being a Christian convert—in fact a catechist—he could not marry a second wife. But he was not the kind of man who carried his sorrow on his face. In particular, he would not let the heathen know that he was unhappy. He had called his fourth daughter Nwanyidinma—"a girl is also good." But his voice did not carry conviction.

The old man who broke the kola nuts in Lagos and called Obi Okonkwo an only palm-fruit was not, however, thinking of Okonkwo's family. He was thinking of the ancient and warlike village of Umuofia. Six or seven years ago Umuofians abroad had formed their Union with the aim of collecting money to send some of their brighter young men to study in England. They taxed themselves mercilessly. The first scholarship under this scheme was awarded to Obi Okonkwo five years ago, almost to the day. Although they called it a scholarship it was to be repaid. In Obi's case it was worth eight hundred pounds, to be repaid within four years of his return. They wanted him to read law so that when he returned he would handle all their land cases against their neighbors. But when he got to England he read English; his self-will was not new. The Union was angry but in the end they left him alone. Although he would not be a lawyer, he would get a "European post" in the civil service.

The selection of the first candidate had not presented any difficulty to the Union. Obi was an obvious choice. At the age of twelve or thirteen he had passed his Standard Six examination at the top of the whole province. Then he had won a scholarship to one of the best secondary schools in Eastern Nigeria. At the end of five years he passed the Cambridge School Certificate with distinction in all eight subjects. He was in fact a village celebrity, and his name was regularly invoked at the mission school where he had once been a pupil. (No one mentioned nowadays that he once brought shame to the school by writing a letter to Adolf Hitler during the war. The headmaster at the time had pointed out, almost in tears, that he was a disgrace to the British Empire, and that if he had been older he would surely have been sent to jail for the rest of his miserable life. He was only eleven then, and so got off with six strokes of the cane on his buttocks.)

Obi's going to England caused a big stir in Umuofia. A few days before his departure to Lagos his parents called a prayer meeting at their home. The Reverend Samuel Ikedi of St. Mark's Anglican Church, Umuofia, was chairman. He said the occasion was the fulfillment of the prophecy:

> "The people which sat in darkness
> Saw a great light,
> And to them which sat in the region
> and shadow of death
> To them did light spring up."

He spoke for over half an hour. Then he asked that someone should lead them in prayer. Mary at once took up the challenge before most people had had time to stand up, let alone shut their eyes. Mary was one of the most zealous Christians in Umuofia and a good friend of Obi's mother, Hannah Okonkwo. Although Mary lived a long way from the church—three miles or more—she never missed the early morning prayer which the pastor conducted at cockcrow. In the heart of the wet season, or the cold harmattan, Mary was sure to be there. Sometimes she came as much as an hour before time. She would blow out her hurricane lamp to save kerosene and go to sleep on the long mud seats.

"Oh, God of Abraham, God of Isaac and God of Jacob," she burst forth, "the Beginning and the End. Without you we can do nothing. The great river is not big enough for you to wash your hands in. You have the yam and you have the knife; we cannot eat unless you cut us a piece. We are like ants in your sight. We are like little children who only wash their stomach when they bathe, leaving their back dry . . ." She went on and on reeling off proverb after proverb and painting picture after picture. Finally, she got round to the subject of the gathering and dealt with it as fully as it deserved, giving among other things, the life history of her friend's son who was about to go to the place where learning finally came to an end. When she was done, people blinked and rubbed their eyes to get used to the evening light once more.

They sat on long wooden forms which had been borrowed from the school. The chairman had a little table before him. On one side sat Obi in his school blazer and white trousers.

Two stalwarts emerged from the kitchen area, half bent with the gigantic iron pot of rice which they carried between them. Another pot followed. Two young women then brought in a simmering pot of stew hot from the fire. Kegs of palm wine followed, and a pile of plates and spoons which the church stocked for the use of its members at marriages, births, deaths, and other occasions such as this.

Mr. Isaac Okonkwo made a short speech placing "this small kola" before his guests. By Umuofia standards he was well-to-do. He had been a catechist of the Church Missionary Society for twenty-five years and then retired on a pension of twenty-five pounds a year. He had been the very first man to build a "zinc" house in Umuofia. It was therefore not unexpected that he would prepare a feast. But no one had imagined anything on this scale, not even from Okonkwo, who was famous for his open-handedness which sometimes bordered on improvidence. Whenever his wife remonstrated against his thriftlessness he replied that a man who lived on the banks of the Niger should not wash his hands with spittle—a favorite saying of his father's. It was odd that he should have rejected everything about his father except this one proverb. Perhaps he had long forgotten that his father often used it.

At the end of the feast the pastor made another long speech. He thanked Okonkwo for giving them a feast greater than many a wedding feast these days.

Mr. Ikedi had come to Umuofia from a township, and was able to tell the gathering how wedding feasts had been steadily declining in the towns since the invention of invitation cards. Many of his hearers whistled in unbelief when he told them that a man could not go to his neighbor's wedding unless he was given one of these papers on which they wrote R.S.V.P.—Rice and Stew Very Plenty— which was invariably an overstatement.

Then he turned to the young man on his right. "In times past," he told him, "Umuofia would have required of you to fight in her wars and bring home human heads. But those were days of darkness from which we have been delivered by the blood of the Lamb of God. Today we send you to bring knowledge. Remember that the fear of the Lord is the beginning of wisdom. I have heard of young men from other towns who went to the white man's country, but instead of facing their studies they went after the sweet things of the flesh. Some of them even married white women." The crowd murmured its strong disapproval of such behavior. "A man who does that is lost to his people. He is like rain wasted in the forest. I would have suggested getting you a wife before you leave. But the time is too short now. Anyway, I know that we have no fear where you are concerned. We are sending you to learn book. Enjoyment can wait. Do not be in a hurry to rush into the pleasures of the world like the young antelope who danced herself lame when the main dance was yet to come."

He thanked Okonkwo again, and the guests for answering his call. "If you had not answered his call, our brother would have become like the king in the Holy Book who called a wedding feast."

As soon as he had finished speaking, Mary raised a song which the women had learnt at their prayer meeting.

> "Leave me not behind Jesus, wait for me
> When I am going to the farm.
> Leave me not behind Jesus, wait for me
> When I am going to the market.
> Leave me not behind Jesus, wait for me
> When I am eating my food.
> Leave me not behind Jesus, wait for me
> When I am having my bath.
> Leave me not behind Jesus, wait for me
> When he is going to the White Man's Country.
> Leave him not behind Jesus, wait for him."

The gathering ended with the singing of "Praise God from whom all blessings flow." The guests then said their farewells to Obi, many of them repeating all the advice that he had already been given. They shook hands with him and as they did so they pressed their presents into his palm, to buy a pencil with, or an exercise book or a loaf of bread for the journey, a shilling there and a penny there—substantial presents in a village where money was so rare, where men and women toiled from year to year to wrest a meager living from an unwilling and exhausted soil.

CHAPTER TWO

OBI WAS AWAY IN ENGLAND FOR A LITTLE UNDER FOUR years. He sometimes found it difficult to believe that it was as short as that. It seemed more like a decade than four years, what with the miseries of winter when his longing to return home took on the sharpness of physical pain. It was in England that Nigeria first became more than just a name to him. That was the first great thing that England did for him.

But the Nigeria he returned to was in many ways different from the picture he had carried in his mind during those four years. There were many things he could no longer recognize, and others—like the slums of Lagos—which he was seeing for the first time.

As a boy in the village of Umuofia he had heard his first stories about Lagos from a soldier home on leave from the war. Those soldiers were heroes who had seen the great world. They spoke of Abyssinia, Egypt, Palestine, Burma and so on. Some of them had been village ne'er-do-wells, but now they were heroes. They had bags and bags of money, and the villagers sat at their feet to listen to their stories. One of them went regularly to a market in the neighboring village and helped himself to whatever he liked. He went in full uniform, breaking the earth with his boots, and no one dared touch him. It was said that if you touched a soldier, Government would deal with you. Besides, soldiers were as strong as lions because of the injections they were given in the army. It was from one of these soldiers that Obi had his first picture of Lagos.

"There is no darkness there," he told his admiring listeners, "because at night the electric shines like the sun, and people are always walking about, that is, those who want to walk. If you don't want to walk you only have to wave your hand and a pleasure car stops for you." His audience made sounds of wonderment. Then by way of digression he said: "If you see a white man, take off your hat for him. The only thing he cannot do is mold a human being."

For many years afterwards, Lagos was always associated with electric lights and motorcars in Obi's mind. Even after he had at last visited the city and spent a few days there before flying to the United Kingdom his views did not change very much. Of course, he did not really see much of Lagos then. His mind was, as it were, on higher things. He spent the few days with his "countryman," Joseph Okeke, a clerk in the Survey Department. Obi and Joseph had been classmates at the Umuofia C.M.S. Central School. But Joseph had not gone on to a secondary school because he was too old and his parents were poor. He had joined the Education Corps of the 82nd Division and, when the war ended, the clerical service of the Nigerian Government.

Joseph was at Lagos Motor Park to meet his lucky

friend who was passing through Lagos to the United Kingdom. He took him to his lodgings in Obalende. It was only one room. A curtain of light-blue cloth ran the full breadth of the room separating the Holy of Holies (as he called his double spring bed) from the sitting area. His cooking utensils, boxes, and other personal effects were hidden away under the Holy of Holies. The sitting area was taken up with two armchairs, a settee (otherwise called "me and my girl"), and a round table on which he displayed his photo album. At night, his houseboy moved away the round table and spread his mat on the floor.

Joseph had so much to tell Obi on his first night in Lagos that it was past three when they slept. He told him about the cinema and the dance halls and about political meetings.

"Dancing is very important nowadays. No girl will look at you if you can't dance. I first met Joy at the dancing school." "Who is Joy?" asked Obi, who was fascinated by what he was learning of this strange and sinful new world. "She was my girl friend for—let's see. . ."—he counted off his fingers— ". . . March, April, May, June, July—for five months. She made these pillowcases for me."

Obi raised himself instinctively to look at the pillow he was lying on. He had taken particular notice of it earlier in the day. It had the strange word *osculate* sewn on it, each letter in a different color.

"She was a nice girl but sometimes very foolish. Sometimes, though, I wish we hadn't broken up. She was simply mad about me; and she was a virgin when I met her, which is very rare here."

Joseph talked and talked and finally became less and less coherent. Then without any pause at all his talk was transformed into a deep snore, which continued until the morning.

The very next day Obi found himself taking a compulsory walk down Lewis Street. Joseph had brought a woman home and it was quite clear that Obi's presence in the room was not desirable; so he went out to have a look round. The girl was one of Joseph's new finds, as he told him later. She was dark and tall with an enormous pneumatic bosom under a tight-fitting red and yellow dress. Her lips and long fingernails were a brilliant red, and her eyebrows were fine black lines. She looked not unlike those wooden masks made in Ikot Ekpene. Altogether she left a nasty taste in Obi's mouth, like the multicolored word *osculate* on the pillowcase.

Some years later as Obi, newly returned from England, stood beside his car at night in one of the less formidable of Lagos slum areas waiting for Clara to take yards of material to her seamstress, his mind went over his earlier impressions of the city. He had not thought places like this stood side by side with the cars, electric lights, and brightly dressed girls.

His car was parked close to a wide-open storm drain from which came a very strong smell of rotting flesh. It was the remains of a dog which had no doubt been run over by a taxi. Obi used to wonder why so many dogs were killed by cars in Lagos, until one day the driver he had engaged to teach him driving went out of his way to run over one. In shocked amazement Obi asked why he had done it. "Na good luck," said the man. "Dog bring good luck for new car. But duck be different. If you kill duck you go get accident or kill man."

Beyond the storm drain there was a meat stall. It was quite empty of meat or meat-sellers. But a man was working a little machine on one of the tables. It looked like a sewing machine except that it ground maize. A woman stood by watching the man turn the machine to grind her maize.

On the other side of the road a little boy wrapped in a cloth was selling bean cakes or *akara* under a lamppost. His bowl of *akara* was lying in the dust and he seemed half asleep. But he really wasn't, for as soon as the night-soilman passed swinging his broom and hurricane lamp and trailing clouds of putrefaction the boy quickly sprang to his feet and began calling him names. The man made for him with his broom but the boy was already in flight, his bowl of *akara* on his head. The man grinding maize burst into laughter, and the woman joined in. The night-soilman smiled and went his way, having said something very rude about the boy's mother.

Here was Lagos, thought Obi, the real Lagos he hadn't imagined existed until now. During his first winter in England he had written a callow, nostalgic poem about Nigeria. It wasn't about Lagos in particular, but Lagos was part of the Nigeria he had in mind.

> "How sweet it is to lie beneath a tree
> At eventime and share the ecstasy
> Of jocund birds and flimsy butterflies;
> How sweet to leave our earthbound body in its mud,
> And rise towards the music of the spheres,
> Descending softly with the wind,
> And the tender glow of the fading sun."

He recalled this poem and then turned and looked at the rotting dog in the storm drain and smiled. "I have tasted putrid flesh in the spoon," he said through clenched teeth. "Far more apt." At last Clara emerged from the side street and they drove away.

They drove for a while in silence through narrow over-crowded streets. "I can't understand why you should choose your dressmaker from the slums." Clara did not reply. Instead she started humming *"Che sarà sarà."*

The streets were now quite noisy and crowded, which was to be expected on a Saturday night at nine o'clock. Every few yards one met bands of dancers often wearing identical dress or *"aso ebi."* Gay temporary sheds were erected in front of derelict houses and lit with brilliant fluorescent tubes for the celebration of an engagement or marriage or birth or promotion or success in business or the death of an old relative.

Obi slowed down as he approached three drummers and a large group of young women in damask and velvet swivelling their waists as effortlessly as oiled ball bearings. A taxi driver hooted impatiently and overtook him, leaning out at the same time to shout: *"Ori oda,* your head no correct!" *"Ori oda*—bloody fool!" replied Obi. Almost immediately a cyclist crossed the road without looking back or giving any signal. Obi jammed on his brakes and his tires screamed on the tarmac. Clara let out a little scream and gripped his left arm. The cyclist looked back once and rode away, his ambition written for all to see on his black bicycle bag—*FUTURE MINISTER.*

Going from the Lagos mainland to Ikoyi on a Saturday night was like going from a bazaar to a funeral. And the vast Lagos cemetery which separated the two places helped to deepen this feeling. For all its luxurious bungalows and flats and its extensive greenery, Ikoyi was like a graveyard. It had no corporate life—at any rate for those Africans who lived there. They had not always lived there, of course. It was once a European reserve. But things had changed, and some Africans in "European posts" had been given houses in Ikoyi. Obi Okonkwo, for example lived there, and as he drove from Lagos to his flat he was struck again by these two cities in one. It always reminded him of twin kernels separated by a thin wall in a palm-nut shell. Sometimes one kernel was shiny black and alive, the other powdery white and dead.

"What is making you so moody?" He looked sideways at Clara, who was ostentatiously sitting as far away from him as she could, pressed against the left door. She did not answer. "Tell me, darling," he said, holding her hand in one of his while he drove with the other. "Leave me, *ojare,*" she said, snatching her hand away.

Obi knew very well why she was moody. She had

suggested in her tentative way that they should go to the films. At this stage in their relationship, Clara never said: "Let us go to films." She said instead: "There is a good film at the Capitol." Obi, who did not care for films, especially those that Clara called good, had said after a long silence: "Well, if you insist, but I'm not keen." Clara did not insist, but she felt very much hurt. All evening she had been nursing her feelings. "It's not too late to go to your film," said Obi, capitulating, or appearing to do so. "You may go if you want to, I'm not coming," she said. Only three days before they had gone to see "a very good film" which infuriated Obi so much that he stopped looking at the screen altogether, except when Clara whispered one explanation or another for his benefit. "That man is going to be killed," she would prophesy, and sure as death, the doomed man would be shot almost immediately. From downstairs the shilling-ticket audience participated noisily in the action.

It never ceased to amaze Obi that Clara should take so much delight in these orgies of killing on the screen. Actually it rather amused him when he thought of it outside the cinema. But while he was there he could feel nothing but annoyance. Clara was well aware of this, and tried her best to ease the tedium for him by squeezing his arm or biting his ear after whispering something into it. "And after all," she would say sometimes, "I don't quarrel with you when you start reading your poems to me." Which was quite true. Only that very morning he had rung her up at the hospital and asked her to come to lunch to meet one of his friends who had recently come to Lagos on transfer from Enugu. Actually Clara had seen the fellow before and didn't like him. So she had said over the telephone that she wasn't keen on meeting him again. But Obi was insistent, and Clara had said: "I don't know why you should want me to meet people that I don't want to meet." "You know, you are a poet, Clara," said Obi.

"To meet people you don't want to meet, that's pure T. S. Eliot."

Clara had no idea what he was talking about but she went to lunch and met Obi's friend, Christopher. So the least that Obi could do in return was to sit through her "very good film," just as she had sat through a very dull lunch while Obi and Christopher theorized about bribery in Nigeria's public life. Whenever Obi and Christopher met they were bound to argue very heatedly about Nigeria's future. Whichever line Obi took, Christopher had to take the opposite. Christopher was an economist from the London School of Economics and he always pointed out that Obi's arguments were not based on factual or scientific analysis, which was not surprising since he had taken a degree in English.

"The civil service is corrupt because of these so-called experienced men at the top," said Obi.

"You don't believe in experience? You think that a chap straight from university should be made a permanent secretary?"

"I didn't say *straight* from the university, but even that would be better than filling our top posts with old men who have no intellectual foundations to support their experience."

"What about the Land Officer jailed last year? *He* is straight from the university."

"He is an exception," said Obi. "But take one of these old men. He probably left school thirty years ago in Standard Six. He has worked steadily to the top through bribery—an ordeal by bribery. To him the bribe is natural. He gave it and he expects it. Our people say that if you pay homage to the man on top, others will pay homage to you when it is your turn to be on top. Well, that is what the old men say."

"What do the young men say, if I may ask?"

"To most of them bribery is no problem. They come straight to the top without bribing anyone. It's not that they're necessarily better than others, it's simply that they can afford to be virtuous. But even that kind of virtue can become a habit."

"Very well put," conceded Christopher as he took a large piece of meat from the *egusi* soup. They were eating pounded yams and *egusi* soup with their fingers. The second generation of educated Nigerians had gone back to eating pounded yams or *garri* with their fingers for the good reason that it tasted better that way. Also for the even better reason that they were not as scared as the first generation of being called uncivilized.

"Zacchaeus!" called Clara.

"Yes, madam," answered a voice from the pantry.

"Bring us more soup."

Zacchaeus had half a mind not to reply, but he thought better of it and said grudgingly: "Yes, madam." Zacchaeus had made up his mind to resign as soon as Master married Madam. "I like Master too much, but this Madam no good," was his verdict.

CHAPTER THREE

THE AFFAIR BETWEEN OBI AND CLARA COULD NOT strictly be called love at first sight. They met at a dance organized by the London branch of the National Council of Nigeria and the Cameroons at the St. Pancras Town Hall. Clara had come with a student who was fairly well known to Obi and who introduced them. Obi was immediately struck by her beauty and followed her with his eyes round the hall. In the end he succeeded in getting a dance with her. But he was so flustered that the only thing he could find to say was: "Have you been dancing very long?" "No. Why?" was the curt reply. Obi was never a very good dancer, but that night he was simply appalling. He stepped on her toes about four times in the first half-minute. Thereafter she concentrated all her attention on moving her foot sideways just in time. As soon as the dance ended she fled. Obi pursued her to her seat to say: "Thank you very much." She nodded without looking.

They did not meet again until almost eighteen months later at the Harrington Dock in Liverpool. For it happened that they were returning to Nigeria the same day on the same boat.

It was a small cargo boat carrying twelve passengers and a crew of fifty. When Obi arrived at the dock the other passengers had all embarked and completed their customs formalities. The short bald-headed customs officer was very friendly. He began by asking Obi whether he had had a happy stay in England. Did he go to a university in England? He must have found the weather very cold.

"I didn't mind the weather very much in the end," said Obi, who had learnt that an Englishman might grumble about his weather but did not expect a foreigner to join in.

When he went into the lounge Obi nearly fell over himself at the sight of Clara. She was talking to an elderly woman and a young Englishman. Obi sat with them and introduced himself. The elderly woman, whose name was Mrs. Wright, was returning to Freetown. The young man was called Macmillan, an administrative officer in Northern Nigeria. Clara introduced herself as Miss Okeke. "I think we have met before," said Obi. Clara looked surprised and somewhat hostile. "At the N.C.N.C. dance in London." "I see," she said, with as much interest as if she had just been told that they were on a boat in the Liverpool Docks, and resumed her conversation with Mrs. Wright.

The boat left the docks at 11 A.M. For the rest of the day Obi kept to himself, watching the sea or reading in his cabin. It was his first sea voyage, and he had already decided that it was infinitely better than flying.

He woke up the following morning without any sign of the much talked about seasickness. He had a warm bath before any of the other passengers were up, and went to the rails to look at the sea. Last evening it had been so placid. Now it had become an endless waste of restless, saggy hillocks topped with white. Obi stood at the rails for nearly an hour drinking in the unspoilt air. "They that go down to the sea in ships . . ." he remembered. He had very little religion nowadays, but he was nevertheless deeply moved.

When the gong sounded for breakfast his appetite was as keen as the morning air. The seating arrangement had been fixed on the previous day. There was a big central table which seated ten, and six little two-seaters ranged round the room. Eight of the twelve passengers sat on the middle table with the captain at the head and the chief engineer at the other end. Obi sat between Macmillan and a Nigerian civil servant called Stephen Udom. Directly in front of him was Mr. Jones, who was something or other in the United Africa Company. Mr. Jones always worked solidly through four of the five heavy courses and then announced to the steward with self-righteous continence: "Just coffee," with the emphasis on the "just."

In contrast to Mr. Jones, the chief engineer hardly touched his food. Watching his face, one would think they had served him portions of Epsom Salts, rhubarb, and *nist. alba.* He held his shoulders up, his arms pressed against his sides as though he was in constant fear of evacuating.

Clara sat on Mr. Jones's left, but Obi studiously refused to look in her direction. She was talking with an Education Officer from Ibadan who was explaining to her the difference between language and dialect.

At first the Bay of Biscay was very calm and collected
The boat was now heading towards a horizon where th
sky was light, seeming to hold out a vague promise c
sunshine. The sea's circumference was no longer merge
with the sky, but stood out in deep clear contrast like
giant tarmac from which God's aeroplane might take of
Then as evening approached, the peace and smoothnes
vanished quite suddenly. The sea's face was contorte
with anger. Obi felt slightly dizzy and top-heavy. When h
went down for supper he merely looked at his food. On
or two passengers were not there at all. The others at
almost in silence.

Obi returned to his cabin and was going straight to be
when someone tapped at his door. He opened and it wa
Clara.

"I noticed you were not looking very well," she said i
Ibo, "so I brought you some tablets of Avomine." Sh
gave him an envelope with half a dozen white tablets in i
"Take two before you go to bed."

"Thank you *very* much. It's so kind of you." Obi wa
completely overwhelmed and all the coldness and indiffer
ence he had rehearsed deserted him. "But," he stam
mered, "am I not depriving you of er . . ."

"Oh, no. I've got enough for all the passengers, that'
the advantage of having a nurse on board." She smile
faintly. "I've just given some to Mrs. Wright and Mr
Macmillan. Good night, you'll feel better in the morning.'

All night Obi rolled from one edge of the bed to th
other in sympathy with the fitful progress of the little shij
groaning and creaking in the darkness. He could neithe
sleep nor keep awake. But somehow he was able to thinl
about Clara most of the night, a few seconds at a time. H
had taken a firm decision not to show any interest in her
And yet when he had opened the door and seen her, hi
joy and confusion must have been very plain. And sh
had treated him just like another patient. "I have enough
for all the passengers," she had said. "I gave some to Mr

Macmillan and Mrs. Wright." But then she had spoken in Ibo, for the first time, as if to say, "We belong together: we speak the same language." And she had appeared to show some concern.

He was up very early next morning, feeling a little better but not yet really well. The crew had already washed the deck and he almost slipped on the wet wood. He took up his favorite position at the rails. Then he heard a woman's light footsteps, turned round, and saw it was Clara.

"Good morning," he said, smiling broadly.

"Good morning," she said, and made to pass.

"Thank you for the tablets," he said in Ibo.

"Did they make you feel better?" she asked in English.

"Yes, very much."

"I am glad," she said, and passed.

Obi leaned again on the rail to watch the restless sea, which now looked like a wilderness, rock-sharp, angular and mobile. For the first time since they had left Liverpool, the sea became really blue; a plumbless blue set off by the gleaming white tops of countless wavelets clashing and breaking against each other. He heard someone treading heavily and briskly and then fall. It was Macmillan.

"I'm sorry," he said.

"Oh, it's nothing," the other said, laughing foolishly and dusting the wet seat of his trousers.

"I very nearly fell myself," said Obi.

"Look out, Miss Okeke," said Macmillan as Clara came round again. "The deck is very treacherous and I've just fallen." He was still dusting his wet seat.

"The captain said we will reach an island tomorrow," said Clara.

"Yes, the Madeiras," said Macmillan. "Tomorrow evening, I think."

"And about time, too," said Obi.

"Don't you like the sea?"

"Yes, but after five days I want a change."

Obi Okonkwo and John Macmillan suddenly became
friends—from the minute Macmillan fell on the wet deck.
They were soon playing ping-pong together and standing
each other drinks.

"What will you have, Mr. Okonkwo?" asked Macmillan.

"Beer, please. It's getting rather warm." He drew his
thumb across his face and flicked the sweat away.

"Isn't it?" said Macmillan, blowing into his chest.
"What's your first name, by the way? Mine's John."

"Obi is mine."

"Obi, that's a fine name. What does it mean? I'm told
that all African names mean something."

"Well, I don't know about *African* names—Ibo names,
yes. They are often long sentences. Like that prophet in
the Bible who called his son The Remnant Shall Return."

"What did you read in London?"

"English. Why?"

"Oh, I just wondered. And how old are you? Excuse
my being so inquisitive."

"Twenty-five," said Obi. "And you?"

"Now that's strange, because I'm twenty-five. How old
do you think Miss Okeke is?"

"Women and music should not be dated," Obi said,
smiling. "I should say about twenty-three."

"She is very beautiful, don't you think?"

"Oh, yes, she is indeed."

The Madeiras were now quite close; two hours or so
someone said. Everyone was at the rails standing one
another drinks. Mr. Jones suddenly became poetic.
"Water, water everywhere but not a drop to drink," he
intoned. Then he became prosaic. "What a waste of
water!" he said.

It struck Obi suddenly that it was true. What a waste of
water. A microscopic fraction of the Atlantic would turn
the Sahara into a flourishing grassland. So much for the

best of all possible worlds. Excess here and nothing at all there.

The ship anchored at Funchal at sunset. A tiny boat came alongside with a young man at the oars and two boys in it. The younger could not have been more than ten; the other was perhaps two years older. They wanted to dive for money. Immediately the coins were flying into the sea from the high deck. The boys picked up every one of them. Stephen Udom threw a penny. They did not move; they did not dive for pennies, they said. Everyone laughed.

As the sun set, the rugged hills of Funchal and the green trees and the houses with their white walls and red tiles looked like an enchanted isle. As soon as dinner was over Macmillan, Obi and Clara went ashore together. They walked on cobbled streets, past quaint cars in the taxi rank. They passed two oxen pulling a cart which was just a flat board on wheels with a man and a sack of something in it. They went into little gardens and parks.

"It's a garden city!" said Clara.

After about an hour they came round to the waterfront again. They sat under a huge red and green umbrella and ordered coffee and wine. A man came round and sold them postcards and then sat down to tell them about Madeira wine. He had very few English words, but he left no one in doubt as to what he meant.

"Las Palmas wine and Italian wine pure water. Madeira wine, two eyes, four eyes." They laughed and he laughed. Then he sold Macmillan tawdy trinkets which everyone knew would tarnish before they got back to their ship.

"Your girl friend won't like it, Mr. Macmillan," said Clara.

"It's for my steward's wife," he explained. And then he added: "I hate to be called Mr. Macmillan. It makes me feel so old."

"I'm sorry," she said. "It's John, isn't it? And you are Obi. I am Clara."

At ten they rose to go because their ship would sail at eleven, or so the captain said. Macmillan discovered he still had some Portuguese coins and ordered another glass of wine, which he shared with Obi. Then they went back to the ship, Macmillan holding Clara's right hand and Obi her left.

The other passengers had not returned and the ship looked deserted. They leaned on the rail and spoke about Funchal. Then Macmillan said he had an important letter to write home. "See you in the morning," he said.

"I think I should write letters, too," said Clara.

"To England?" asked Obi.

"No, to Nigeria."

"There's no hurry," he said, "you can't post Nigerian letters until you get to Freetown. That's what they said."

They heard Macmillan bang his cabin door. Their eyes met for a second, and without another word Obi took her in his arms. She was trembling as he kissed her over and over again.

"Leave me," she whispered.

"I love you."

She was silent for a while, seeming to melt in his arms.

"You don't," she said suddenly. "We're only being silly. You'll forget it in the morning." She looked at him and then kissed him violently. "I know I'll hate myself in the morning. You don't—— Leave me, there's someone coming."

It was Mrs. Wright, the African lady from Freetown.

"Have you come back?" she asked. "Where are the others? I have not been able to sleep." She had indigestion, she said.

CHAPTER FOUR

UNLIKE MAIL BOATS, WHICH DOCKED AT THE LAGOS WHARF on fixed days of the week, cargo boats were most unpredictable. So when the MV *Sasa* arrived, there were no friends waiting at the Atlantic Terminal for her passengers. On mail boat days the beautiful and airy waiting room would be full of gaily dressed friends and relations waiting for the arrival of a boat and drinking iced beer and Coca-Cola or eating buns. Sometimes you found a little group waiting sadly and silently. In such cases you could bet that their son had married a white woman in England.

There was no such crowd for the MV *Sasa*, and it was quite clear that Mr. Stephen Udom was deeply disappointed. As soon as Lagos had been sighted he had returned to his cabin to emerge half an hour later in a black suit, bowler hat, and rolled umbrella, even though it was a hot October day.

Customs formalities here took thrice as long as at Liverpool and five times as many officials. A young man, almost a boy in fact, was dealing with Obi's cabin. He told him that the duty on his radiogram would be five pounds.

"Right," said Obi, feeling his hip pockets. "Write a receipt for me." The boy did not write. He looked at Obi for a few seconds, and then said: "I can be able to reduce it to two pounds for you."

"How?" asked Obi.

"I fit do it, but you no go get Government receipt."

35

For a few seconds Obi was speechless. Then he merely said: "Don't be silly. If there was a policeman here I would hand you over to him." The boy fled from his cabin without another word. Obi found him later attending other passengers.

"Dear old Nigeria," he said to himself as he waited for another official to come to his cabin. In the end one came when all the other passengers had been attended to.

If Obi had returned by mail boat, the Umuofia Progressive Union (Lagos Branch) would have given him a royal welcome at the harbor. Anyhow, it was decided at their meeting that a big reception should be arranged to which press reporters and photographers should be invited. An invitation was also sent to the Nigerian Broadcasting Service to cover the occasion and to record the Umuofia Ladies' Vocal Orchestra, which had been learning a number of new songs.

The reception took place on Saturday afternoon at 4 P.M. on Moloney Street, where the President had two rooms.

Everybody was properly dressed in *aghada* or European suit except the guest of honor, who appeared in his shirtsleeves because of the heat. That was Obi's mistake Number One. Everybody expected a young man from England to be impressively turned out.

After prayers the Secretary of the Union read the Welcome Address. He rose, cleared his throat, and began to intone from an enormous sheet of paper.

"Welcome Address presented to Michael Obi Okonkwo, B.A. (Hons), London, by the officers and members of the Umuofia Progressive Union on the occasion of his return from the United Kingdom in quest of the Golden Fleece.

"Sir, we the officers and members of the above-named Union present with humility and gratitude this token of our appreciation of your unprecedented academic brilliance. . . ."

He spoke of the great honor Obi had brought to the ancient town of Umuofia, which could now join the comity of other towns in their march towards political irredentism, social equality, and economic emancipation.

"The importance of having one of our sons in the vanguard of this march of progress is nothing short of axiomatic. Our people have a saying 'Ours is ours, but mine is mine.' Every town and village struggles at this momentous epoch in our political evolution to possess that of which it can say: 'This is mine.' We are happy that today we have such an invaluable possession in the person of our illustrious son and guest of honor."

He traced the history of the Umuofia Scholarship Scheme, which had made it possible for Obi to study overseas, and called it an investment which must yield heavy dividends. He then referred (quite obliquely, of course) to the arrangement whereby the beneficiary from this scheme was expected to repay his debt over four years so that "an endless stream of students will be enabled to drink deep at the Pierian Spring of knowledge."

Needless to say, this address was repeatedly interrupted by cheers and the clapping of hands. What a sharp young man their secretary was, all said. He deserved to go to England himself. He wrote the kind of English they admired if not understood: the kind that filled the mouth, like the proverbial dry meat.

Obi's English, on the other hand, was most unimpressive. He spoke "is" and "was." He told them about the value of education. "Education for service, not for white-collar jobs and comfortable salaries. With our great country on the threshold of independence, we need men who are prepared to serve her well and truly."

When he sat down the audience clapped from politeness. Mistake Number Two.

Cold beer, minerals, palm-wine, and biscuits were then served, and the women began to sing about Umuofia and about Obi Okonkwo *nwa jelu oyibo*—Obi who had been to the land of the whites. The refrain said over and over again that the power of the leopard resided in its claws.

"Have they given you a job yet?" the chairman asked Obi over the music. In Nigeria the government was "they." It had nothing to do with you or me. It was an alien institution and people's business was to get as much from it as they could without getting into trouble.

"Not yet. I'm attending an interview on Monday."

"Of course those of you who know book will not have any difficulty," said the Vice-President on Obi's left. "Otherwise I would have suggested *seeing* some of the men beforehand."

"It would not be necessary," said the President, "since they would be mostly white men."

"You think white men don't eat bribe? Come to our department. They eat more than black men nowadays."

After the reception Joseph took Obi to have dinner at the "Palm Grove." It was a neat little place, not very popular on Saturday nights, when Lagosians wanted a more robust kind of enjoyment. There were a handful of people in the lounge—a dozen or so Europeans and three Africans.

"Who owns this place?"

"I think a Syrian. They own everything in Lagos," said Joseph.

They sat at one of the empty tables at the corner and then noticed that they were directly under a ceiling fan and moved to another table. Soft light came from large globes around which insects danced furiously. Perhaps they did not notice that each globe carried a large number of bodies which, like themselves, had danced once upon a time. Or if they noticed, they did not care.

"Service!" called Joseph importantly, and a steward appeared in white tunic and trousers, a red cummerbund and red fez. "What will you have?" he asked Obi. The steward bent forward waiting.

"Really, I don't think I want to drink anything more."

"Nonsense. The day is still young. Have a cold beer."

He turned to the steward. "Two Heinekens."

"Oh, no. One will do. Let's share one."

"Two Heinekens," repeated Joseph, and the steward went to the bar and soon returned with two bottles on a tray.

"Do they serve Nigerian food here?"

Joseph was surprised at the question. No decent restaurant served Nigerian food. "Do you want Nigerian food?"

"Of course. I have been dying to eat pounded yams and bitter-leaf soup. In England we made do with semolina, but it isn't the same thing."

"I must ask my boy to prepare you pounded yams tomorrow afternoon."

"Good man!" said Obi, brightening up considerably. Then he added in English for the benefit of the European group that sat at the next table: "I am sick of boiled potatoes." By calling them boilèd he hoped he had put into it all the disgust he felt.

A white hand gripped his chair behind. He turned quickly and saw it was the old manageress holding on to chairs to support her unsteady progress. She must have been well over seventy, if not eighty. She toddled across the lounge and behind the counter. Then she came out again holding a shivering glass of milk.

"Who left that duster there?" she said, pointing a shaking left-hand finger at a yellow rag on the floor.

"I no know," said the steward who had been addressed.

"Take it away," she croaked. In the effort to give orders she forgot about the glass of milk. It tilted in her unsteady grip and spilt on her neat floral dress. She went to a seat in the corner and sank in, groaning and creaking like old machinery gone rusty from standing in the rain. It must have been her favorite corner, because her parrot's cage was directly overhead. As soon as she sat down the parrot emerged from its cage on to a projecting rod, lowered its tail, and passed ordure, which missed the old lady by a tenth of an inch. Obi raised himself slightly on his seat to see the mess on the floor. But there was no mess. Everything was beautifully organized. There was a tray by the old lady's chair nearly full of wet excrement.

"I don't think the place is owned by a Syrian," said Obi. "She is English."

They had mixed grill, which Obi admitted wasn't too bad. But he was still puzzling in his mind why Joseph had not put him up as he had asked before he left England. Instead, the Umuofia Progressive Union had arranged at their own expense for him to stay at a not particularly good hotel owned by a Nigerian, on the outskirts of Yaba.

"Did you get my last letter from England?"

Joseph said yes. As soon as he had got it he had discussed it with the executive of the U.P.U., and it was agreed that he should be put up in proper fashion at a hotel. As if he read Obi's thoughts, he said: "You know I have only one room."

"Nonsense," said Obi. "I'm moving out of this filthy hotel tomorrow morning and coming into your place."

Joseph was amazed, but also very pleased. He tried to raise another objection, but it was clear his heart was not in it.

"What will the people of other towns say when they hear that a son of Umuofia returned from England and shared a room in Obalende?"

"Let them say what they like."

They ate in silence for a short while and then Obi said: "Our people have a long way to go." At the same time as he was saying it Joseph was also beginning to say something, but he stopped.

"Yes, you were saying something."

"I said that I believe in destiny."

"Do you? Why?"

"You remember Mr. Anene, our class teacher, used to say that you would go to England. You were so small then with a running nose, and yet at the end of every term you were at the top of the class. You remember we used to call you 'Dictionary'?"

Obi was very much embarrassed because Joseph was talking at the top of his voice.

"As a matter of fact, my nose still runs. They say it's hay fever."

"And then," said Joseph, "you wrote that letter to Hitler."

Obi laughed one of his rare loud laughs. "I wonder what came over me. I still think about it sometimes. What was Hitler to me or I to Hitler? I suppose I felt sorry for him. And I didn't like going into the bush every day to pick palm-kernels as our 'Win the War Effort.' " He suddenly became serious. "And when you come to think of it, it was quite immoral of the headmaster to tell little children every morning that for every palm-kernel they picked they were buying a nail for Hitler's coffin."

They went back to the lounge from the dining room. Joseph was about to order more beer, but Obi stoutly refused.

From where he sat Obi could see cars passing on Broad Street. A long De Soto pulled up exactly at the entrance and a young handsome man walked into the lounge. Everyone turned to look at him and faint sibilant sounds filled the room as each told his neighbor that it was the Minister of State.

"That's Hon Sam Okoli," whispered Joseph. But Obi had suddenly become like one thunderstruck gazing at the De Soto in the half-darkness.

The Honorable Sam Okoli was one of the most popular politicians in Lagos and in Eastern Nigeria where his constituency was. The newspapers called him the best-dressed gentleman in Lagos and the most eligible bachelor. Although he was definitely over thirty, he always looked like a boy just out of school. He was tall and athletic with a flashing smile for all. He walked across to the bar and paid for a tin of Churchman's. All the while

Obi's gaze was fixed on the road outside where Clara lounged in the De Soto. He had only caught a lightning glimpse of her. Perhaps it wasn't her at all. The Minister went back to the car, and as he opened the door the pale interior light again bathed the plush cushions. There was no doubt about it now. It was Clara.

"What's the matter?"

"Nothing. I know that girl, that's all."

"In England?"

Obi nodded.

"Good old Sam! He doesn't spare them."

CHAPTER FIVE

OBI'S THEORY THAT THE PUBLIC SERVICE OF NIGERIA would remain corrupt until the old Africans at the top were replaced by young men from the universities was first formulated in a paper read to the Nigerian Students' Union in London. But unlike most theories formed by students in London, this one survived the first impact of homecoming. In fact, within a month of his return Obi came across two classic examples of his old African.

He met the first one at the Public Service Commission, where he was boarded for a job. Fortunately for Obi, he had already created a favorable impression on the board before this man made him lose his temper.

It happened that the Chairman of the Commission, a fat jolly Englishman, was very keen on modern poetry and the modern novel, and enjoyed talking about them. The other four members—one European and three Africans—

not knowing anything about that side of life, were duly impressed. Or perhaps we should say in strict accuracy that three of them were duly impressed because the fourth was asleep throughout the interview; which on the surface might appear to be quite unimportant had not this gentleman been the sole representative of one of the three regions of Nigeria. (In the interests of Nigerian unity the region shall remain nameless.)

The Chairman's conversation with Obi ranged from Graham Greene to Tutuola and took the greater part of half an hour. Obi said afterwards that he talked a lot of nonsense, but it was a learned and impressive kind of nonsense. He surprised even himself when he began to flow.

"You say you're a great admirer of Graham Greene. What do you think of *The Heart of the Matter*?"

"The only sensible novel any European has written on West Africa and one of the best novels I have read." Obi paused, and then added almost as an afterthought: "Only it was nearly ruined by the happy ending."

The Chairman sat up in his chair.

"Happy ending? Are you sure it's *The Heart of the Matter* you're thinking about? The European police officer commits suicide."

"Perhaps happy ending it too strong, but there is no other way I can put it. The police officer is torn between his love of a woman and his love of God, and he commits suicide. It's much too simple. Tragedy isn't like that at all. I remember an old man in my village, a Christian convert, who suffered one calamity after another. He said life was like a bowl of wormwood which one sips a little at a time world without end. He understood the nature of tragedy."

"You think that suicide ruins a tragedy," said the Chairman.

"Yes. Real tragedy is never resolved. It goes on hopelessly forever. Conventional tragedy is too easy. The hero dies and we feel a purging of the emotions. A real

tragedy takes place in a corner, in an untidy spot, to quote
W. H. Auden. The rest of the world is unaware of it. Like
that man in *A Handful of Dust* who reads Dickens to Mr.
Todd. There is no release for him. When the story ends he
is still reading. There is no purging of the emotions for us
because we are not there."

"That's most interesting," said the Chairman. Then he
looked round the table and asked the other members if
they had any questions for Mr. Okonkwo. They all said
no, except the man who had been sleeping.

"Why do you want a job in the civil service? So that
you can take bribes?" he asked.

Obi hesitated. His first impulse was to say it was an
idiotic question. He said instead: "I don't know how you
expect me to answer that question. Even if my reason is to
take bribes, you don't expect me to admit it before this
board. So I don't think it's a very useful question."

"It's not for you to decide what questions are useful,
Mr. Okonkwo," said the Chairman, trying unsuccessfully
to look severe. "Anyhow, you'll be hearing from us in due
course. Good morning."

Joseph was not very happy when Obi told him the story
of the interview. His opinion was that a man in need of a
job could not afford to be angry.

"Nonsense!" said Obi. "That's what I call colonial mentality."

"Call it what you like," said Joseph in Ibo. "You know
more book than I, but I am older and wiser. And I can
tell you that a man does not challenge his *chi* to a wrestling match."

Joseph's houseboy, Mark, brought in rice and stew and
they immediately fell to. He then went across the street to
a shop where iced water was sold at a penny a bottle and
brought them two bottles, carrying all the way and back a
smudge of soot at the tip of his nose. His eyes were a little
red and watery from blowing the fire with his breath.

"You know you have changed a good deal in four

years," Obi remarked after they had been eating for a while in silence. "Then you had two interests—politics and women."

Joseph smiled. "You don't do politics on an empty stomach."

"Agreed," said Obi jovially. "What about women? I have been two days here now and I haven't seen one yet."

"Didn't I tell you I was getting married?"

"So what?"

"When you have paid a hundred and thirty pounds bride-price and you are only a second-class clerk, you find you haven't got any more to spare on other women."

"You mean you paid a hundred and thirty? What about the bride-price law?"

"It pushed up the price, that's all."

"It's a pity my three elder sisters got married too early for us to make money on them. We'll try and make up on the others."

"It's no laughing matter," said Joseph. "Wait until you want to marry. They will probably ask you to pay five hundred, seeing that you are in the senior service."

"I'm not in the senior service. You have just been telling me that I won't get the job because I told that idiot what I thought of him. Anyway, senior service or no senior service, I'm not paying five hundred pounds for a wife. I shall not even pay one hundred, not even fifty."

"You are not serious," said Joseph. "Unless you are going to be a Reverend Father."

While he waited for the result of his interview, Obi paid a short visit to Umuofia, his home town, five hundred miles away in the Eastern Region. The journey itself was not very exciting. He boarded a mammy wagon called *God's Case No Appeal* and traveled first class; which meant that he shared the front seat with the driver and a young woman with her baby. The back seats were taken up by traders who traveled regularly between Lagos and the famous Onitsha market on the bank of the Niger. The lorry was so heavily laden that the traders had no room to hang their legs down. They sat with their feet on the same level as their buttocks, their knees drawn up to their chins like roast chickens. But they did not seem to mind. They beguiled themselves with gay and bawdy songs addressed mostly to young women who had become nurses or teachers instead of mothers.

The driver of the lorry was a very quiet man. He was either eating kola nuts or smoking cigarettes. The kola was to keep him awake at night because the journey began in the late afternoon, took all night, and ended in the early morning. From time to time he asked Obi to strike a match and light his cigarette for him. Actually it was Obi who offered to do it in the first instance. He had been alarmed to see the man controlling the wheel with his elbows while he fumbled for a match.

Some forty miles or so beyond Ibadan the driver suddenly said: "Dees b—— f—— police!" Obi noticed two policemen by the side of the road about three hundred yards away, signaling the lorry to a stop.

"Your particulars?" said one of them to the driver. It was at this point that Obi noticed that the seat they sat on was also a kind of safe for keeping money and valuable documents. The driver asked his passengers to get up. He unlocked the box and brought out a sheaf of papers. The policeman looked at them critically. "Where your road-worthiness?" The driver showed him his certificate of roadworthiness.

Meanwhile the driver's mate was approaching the other policeman. But just as he was about to hand something over to him Obi looked in their direction. The policeman was not prepared to take a risk; for all he knew Obi might be a C.I.D. man. So he drove the driver's mate away with great moral indignation. "What you want here? Go away!" Meanwhile the other policeman had found fault with the driver's papers and was taking down his particulars, the driver pleading and begging in vain. Finally he drove away, or so it appeared. About a quarter of a mile farther up the road he stopped.

"Why you look the man for face when we want give um him two shillings?" he asked Obi.

"Because he has no right to take two shillings from you," Obi answered.

"Na him make I no de want carry you book people," he complained. "Too too know na him de worry una. Why you put your nose for matter way no concern you? Now that policeman go charge me like ten shillings."

It was only some minutes later that Obi realized why they had stopped. The driver's mate had run back to the policemen, knowing that they would be more amenable when there were no embarrassing strangers gazing at them. The man soon returned panting from much running.

"How much they take?" asked the driver.

"Ten shillings," gasped his assistant.

"You see now," he said to Obi, who was already beginning to feel a little guilty, especially as all the traders behind, having learnt what was happening, had switched their attacks from career girls to "too know" young men. For the rest of the journey the driver said not a word more to him.

"What an Augean stable!" he muttered to himself. "Where does one begin? With the masses? Educate the masses?" He shook his head. "Not a chance there. It would take centuries. A handful of men at the top. Or even one man with vision—an enlightened dictator. People are scared of the word nowadays. But what kind of democracy can exist side by side with so much corruption and ignorance? Perhaps a halfway house—a sort of compromise." When Obi's reasoning reached this point he reminded himself that England had been as corrupt not so very long ago. He was not really in the mood for consecutive reasoning. His mind was impatient to roam in a more pleasant landscape.

The young woman sitting on his left was now asleep, clasping her baby tightly to her breast. She was going to Benin. That was all he knew about her. She hardly spoke a word of English and he did not speak Bini. He shut his eyes and imagined her to be Clara; their knees were touching. It did not work.

Why did Clara insist that he must not tell his people about her yet? Could it be that she had not quite made up her mind to marry him? That could hardly be. She was as anxious as himself to be formally engaged, only she said he should not go to the expense of buying a ring until he had got a job. Perhaps she wanted to tell her people first. But if so, why all the mystery? Why had she not simply said that she was going to consult her people? Or maybe she was not as guileless as he had assumed and was using this suspense to bind him more strongly to her. Obi examined each possibility in turn and rejected it.

As the night advanced the rushing air became at first cool and refreshing and then chilly. The driver pulled out a dirty brown cloth cap from the mass of rags on which he sat and covered his head with it. The young Benin woman retied her headcloth to cover her ears. Obi had an old sports jacket which he had bought in his first year in England. He had used it until now to soften the wooden backrest. He threw it over his back and shoulders. But his feet and legs were now the only really comfortable parts of him. The heat of the engine, which had been a little uncomfortable before, had now been mellowed down by the chilly air until it gently caressed the feet and legs.

Obi was beginning to feel sleepy and his thoughts turned more and more on the erotic. He said words in his mind that he could not say out aloud even when he was alone. Strangely enough, all the words were in his mother tongue. He could say any English word, no matter how dirty, but some Ibo words simply would not proceed from his mouth. It was no doubt his early training that operated this censorship, English words filtering through because they were learnt later in life.

Obi continued in his state of half-asleep until the driver suddenly pulled up by the side of the road, rubbed his eyes, and announced that he had caught himself sleeping once or twice. Everyone was naturally concerned about it and tried to be helpful.

"You no get kola nut for eat?" asked one of the traders from the back.

"Weting I been de eat all afternoon?" asked the driver. "I no fit understand this kind sleep. Na true say I no sleep last night, but that no be first time I been do um." Everyone agreed that sleep was a most unreasonable phenomenon.

After two or three minutes of general conversation on this subject the driver once more proceeded on his way with the promise and determination to try his best. As for Obi, sleep had fled from his eyes as soon as the driver had pulled up. His mind cleared immediately as if the sun had risen and dried the dew that had settled on it.

The traders burst into song again, this time there was nothing bawdy about it. Obi knew the refrain, he tried to translate it into English, and for the first time its real meaning dawned on him.

> "An in-law went to see his in-law
> Oyiemu—o
> His in-law seized him and killed him
> Oyiemu—o
> Bring a canoe, bring a paddle
> Oyiemu—o
> The paddle speaks English
> Oyiemu—o."

On the face of it there was no kind of logic or meaning in the song. But as Obi turned it round and round in his mind, he was struck by the wealth of association that even such a mediocre song could have. First of all it was unheard of for a man to seize his in-law and kill him. To the Ibo mind it was the height of treachery. Did not the elders say that a man's in-law was his *chi*, his personal god? Set against this was another great betrayal; a paddle that begins suddenly to talk in a language which its master, the fisherman, does not understand. In short, then, thought Obi, the burden of the song was "the world turned upside down." He was pleased with his exegesis and began to search in his mind for other songs that could be given the same treatment. But the song of the traders was now so loud and spicy that he could not concentrate on his thinking.

Nowadays going to England has become as commonplace as going down to the village green. But five years ago it was different. Obi's return to his village was almost a festival. A "pleasure" car was waiting at Onitsha to convey him in proper state to Umuofia, some fifty miles away. But before they set out he had a few minutes to look round the great Onitsha market.

The first thing that claimed his attention was an open jeep which blared out local music from a set of loudspeakers. Two men in the car swayed to the music as did many others in the crowd that had gathered round it. Obi was wondering what it was all about when the music suddenly stopped. One of the men held up a bottle for all to see. It contained Long Life Mixture, he said, and began to tell the crowd all about it. Or rather he told them a few things about it, for it was impossible to enumerate all its wonderful virtues. The other man brought out a sheaf of handbills and distributed them to the crowd, most of whom appeared to be illiterate. "This paper will speak to you about Long Life Mixture," he announced. It was quite clear that if there was something on paper about it, then it must be true. Obi secured one of the bills and read the list of diseases. The first three were: "Rheumatism, Yellow fever, dogbight."

On the other side of the road, close to the waterfront, a row of women sat selling *garri* from big white enamel bowls. A beggar appeared. He must have been well known because many people called him by name. Perhaps he was a little mad too. His name was One Way. He had an enamel basin and began a tour of the row. The women beat out a rhythm with empty cigarette cups and One Way danced along the row, receiving a handful of *garri* in his basin from each of them in turn. When he got to the end of the row he had received enough *garri* for two heavy meals.

Bands of music-makers went out two miles on the Umuofia—Onitsha road to await Obi's arrival. There were at least five different groups, if one excludes the brass band of the C.M.S. School Umuofia. It looked as if the entire village was celebrating a feast. Those who were not waiting along the road, elderly people especially, were already arriving in large numbers at Mr. Okonkwo's compound.

The only trouble was that it might rain. In fact, many people half wished it would rain heavily so as to show Isaac Okonkwo that Christianity had made him blind. He was the only man who failed to see that on an occasion such as this he should take palm-wine, a cock, and a little money to the chief rainmaker in Umuofia.

"He is not the only Christian we have seen," said one of the men. "But it is like the palm-wine we drink. Some people can drink it and remain wise. Others lose all their senses."

"Very true, very true," said another. "When a new saying gets to the land of empty men they lose their heads over it."

At that very moment Isaac Okonkwo was having an

argument about rainmaking with one of the old men who had come to rejoice with him.

"Perhaps you will also tell me that some men cannot send thunder to their enemies?" asked the old man.

Mr. Okonkwo told him that to believe such a thing was to chew the cud of foolishness. It was putting one's head into a cooking pot.

"What Satan has accomplished in this world of ours is indeed great," he said. "For it is he alone that can put such abominable thought into men's stomachs."

The old man waited patiently for him to finish and said:

"You are not a stranger in Umuofia. You have heard our elders say that thunder cannot kill a son or daughter of Umuofia. Do you know anyone either now or in the past who was so killed?"

Okonkwo had to admit that he knew of no such person. "But that is the work of God," he said.

"It is the work of our forefathers," said the old man. "They built a powerful medicine to protect themselves from thunder, and not only themselves, but all their descendants forever."

"Very true," said another man. "Anyone who denies it does so in vain. Let him go and ask Nwokeke how he was hit by thunder last year. All his skin peeled off like snake slough, but he was not killed."

"Why was he hit at all?" asked Okonkwo. "He should not have been hit at all."

"That is a matter between him and his *chi*. But you must know that he was hit in Mbaino and not at home. Perhaps the thunder, seeing him at Mbaino, called him an Mbaino man at first."

Four years in England had filled Obi with a longing to be back in Umuofia. This feeling was sometimes so strong that he found himself feeling ashamed of studying English for his degree. He spoke Ibo whenever he had the least opportunity of doing so. Nothing gave him greater plea-

ure than to find another Ibo-speaking student in a London bus. But when he had to speak in English with a
Nigerian student from another tribe he lowered his voice.
t was humiliating to have to speak to one's countryman
n a foreign language, especially in the presence of the
proud owners of that language. They would naturally
assume that one had no language of one's own. He wished
they were here today to see. Let them come to Umuofia
now and listen to the talk of men who made a great art of
onversation. Let them come and see men and women
nd children who knew how to live, whose joy of life had
not yet been killed by those who claimed to teach other
nations how to live.

There were hundreds of people at Obi's reception. For
one thing, the entire staff and pupils of the C.M.S. Central
chool Umuofia were there and their brass band had just
inished playing "Old Calabar." They had also played an
ld evangelical tune which in Obi's schooldays Protestant
choolchildren had sung to anti-Catholic words, especially
n Empire Day, when Protestants and Catholics competed
n athletics.

> *"Otasili osukwu Onyenkuzi Fada*
> *E misisi ya oli awo-o."*

Which translated into English is as follows:

> "Palm-fruit eater, Roman Catholic teacher,
> His missus a devourer of toads."

After the first four hundred handshakes and hundred
mbraces, Obi was able to sit down for a while with his
ather's older kinsmen in the big parlor. There were not
nough chairs for all of them to sit on, so that many sat on
heir goatskins spread on the floor. It did not make much
ifference whether one sat on a chair or on the floor

because even those who sat on chairs spread their goat
skins on them first.

"The white man's country must be very distant in
deed," suggested one of the men. Everyone knew it wa
very distant, but they wanted to hear it again from th
mouth of their young kinsman.

"It is not something that can be told," said Obi. "It too
the white man's ship sixteen days—four market weeks—
to do the journey."

"Think of that," said one of the men to the other
"Four market weeks. And not in a canoe, but a whit
man's ship that runs on water as a snake runs on grass."

"Sometimes for a whole market week there is no land t
be seen," said Obi. "No land in front, behind, to the righ
and to the left. Only water."

"Think of that," said the man to the others. "No lan
for one whole market week. In our folk stories a man get
to the land of spirits when he has passed seven rivers
seven forests, and seven hills. Without doubt you hav
visited the land of spirits."

"Indeed you have, my child," said another old man
"Azik," he called, meaning Isaac, "bring us a kola nut t
break for this child's return."

"This is a Christian house," replied Obi's father.

"A Christian house where kola nut is not eaten?"
sneered the man.

"Kola nut is eaten here," replied Mr. Okonkwo, "bu
not sacrificed to idols."

"Who talked about sacrifice? Here is a little child re
turned from wrestling in the spirit world and you sit ther
blabbing about Christian house and idols, talking like a
man whose palm-wine has gone into his nose." He hisse
in disgust, took up his goat skin, and went to sit outside.

"This is not a day for quarrels," said another old man
"I shall bring a kola nut." He took his goatskin bag whicl
he had hung from his chair and began to search it
depths. As he searched things knocked against one anoth

er in it—his drinking horn, his snuff bottle, and a spoon. "And we shall break it in the Christian way," he said as he fished out a kola nut.

"Do not trouble yourself, Ogbuefi Odogwu," said Okonkwo to him. "I am not refusing to place a kola nut before you. What I say is that it will not be used as a heathen sacrifice in my house." He went into an inner room and soon returned with three kola nuts in a saucer. Ogbuefi Odogwu insisted on adding his kola nut to the number.

"Obi, show the kola nut round," said his father. Obi had already stood up to do so, being the youngest man in the room. When everyone had seen he placed the saucer before Ogbuefi Odogwu, who was the eldest. He was not a Christian, but he knew one or two things about Christianity. Like many others in Umuofia, he went to church once a year at harvest. His only criticism of the Christian service was that the congregation was denied the right to reply to the sermon. One of the things he liked particularly and understood was: "As it was in the beginning, is now and ever shall be, world without end."

"As a man comes into this world," he often said, "so will he go out of it. When a titled man dies, his anklets of title are cut so that he will return as he came. The Christians are right when they say that as it was in the beginning it will be in the end."

He took the saucer, drew up his knees together to form a table, and placed the saucer there. He raised his two hands, palms facing upwards, and said: "Bless this kola nut so that when we eat it it will be good in our body in the name of Jesu Kristi. As it was in the beginning it will be at the end. Amen." Everyone replied Amen and cheered old Odogwu on his performance. Even Okonkwo could not help joining in the cheers.

"You should become a Christian," he suggested.

"Yes, if you will agree to make me a pastor," said Odogwu.

Everyone laughed again. Then the conversation veered round again to Obi. Matthew Ogbonna, who had been a carpenter in Onitsha and was consequently a man of the world, said they should all thank God that Obi had not brought home a white wife.

"White wife?" asked one of the men. To him it was rather farfetched.

"Yes. I have seen it with my two eyes," said Matthew.

"Yes," said Obi. "Many black men who go to the white man's country marry their women."

"You hear?" asked Matthew. "I tell you I have seen it with my own two eyes in Onitsha. The woman even had two children. But what happened in the end? She left those children and went back to her country. That is why I say a black man who marries a white woman wastes his time. Her stay with him is like the stay of the moon in the sky. When the times comes she will go."

"Very true," said another man who had also traveled. "It is not her going away that matters. It is her turning the man's face away from his kinsmen while she stays."

"I am happy that you returned home safe," said Matthew to Obi.

"He is a son of Iguedo," said old Odogwu. "There are nine villages in Umuofia, but Iguedo is Iguedo. We have our faults, but we are not empty men who become white when they see white, and black when they see black."

Obi's heart glowed with pride within him.

"He is the grandson of Ogbuefi Okonkwo who faced the white man single-handed and died in the fight. Stand up!"

Obi stood up obediently.

"Remark him," said Odogwu. "He is Ogbuefi Okonkwo come back. He is Okonkwo *kpom-kwem*, exact, perfect."

Obi's father cleared his throat in embarrassment. "Dead men do not come back," he said.

"I tell you this is Okonkwo. As it was in the beginning so it will be in the end. That is what your religion tells us."

"It does not tell you that dead men return."

"Iguedo breeds great men," said Odogwu, changing the subject. "When I was young I knew of them—Okonkwo, Ezeudu, Obierika, Okolo, Nwosu." He counted them off with his right fingers against the left. "And many others, as many as grains of sand. Among their fathers we hear of Ndu, Nwosisi, Ikedi, Obika, and his brother Iweka—all giants. These men were great in their day. Today greatness has changed its tune. Titles are no longer great, neither are barns or large numbers of wives and children. Greatness is now in the things of the white man. And so we too have changed our tune. We are the first in all the nine villages to send our son to the white man's land. Greatness has belonged to Iguedo from ancient times. It is not made by man. You cannot plant greatness as you plant yams or maize. Who ever planted an iroko tree—the greatest tree in the forest? You may collect all the iroko seeds in the world, open the soil and put them there. It will be in vain. The great tree chooses where to grow and we find it there, so it is with the greatness in men."

CHAPTER SIX

OBI'S HOMECOMING WAS NOT IN THE END THE HAPPY event he had dreamt of. The reason was his mother. She had grown so old and frail in four years that he could hardly believe it. He had heard of her long periods of illness, but he had not thought of it quite this way. Now that all the visitors had gone away and she came and hugged him and put her arms round his neck, for the second time tears rose in his eyes. Henceforth he wore her sadness round his neck like a necklace of stone.

His father too was all bones, although he did not look nearly as bad as his mother. It was clear to Obi that they did not have enough good food to eat. It was scandalous, he thought, that after nearly thirty years' service in the church his father should retire on a salary of two pounds a month, a good slice of which went back to the same church by way of class fees and other contributions. And he had his two last children at school, each paying school fees and church fees.

Obi and his father sat up for a long time after the others had gone to bed, in the oblong room which gave on to the outside through a large central door and two windows. This room was called *pieze* in Christian houses. The door and windows were shut to discourage neighbors who would have continued to stream in to see Obi—some of them for the fourth time that day.

There was a hurricane lamp beside the chair on which Obi's father sat. It was his lamp. He washed the globe himself; he would not trust anybody to do it. The lamp itself was older than Obi.

The walls of the *pieze* had recently been given a new coat of chalk. Obi had not had a moment until now to look round for such loving tributes. The floor had also been rubbed; but what with the countless feet that had trod on it that day it was already needing another rubbing with red earth and water.

His father broke the silence at length.

"Lord, now lettest thou thy servant depart in peace according to thy word."

"What is that, Father?" asked Obi.

"Sometimes fear came upon me that I might not be spared to see your return."

"Why? You seem as strong as ever."

Obi's father ignored the false compliment, pursuing his own train of thought. "Tomorrow we shall all worship at church. The pastor has agreed to make it a special service for you."

"But is it necessary, Father? Is it not enough that we pray together here as we prayed this night?"

"It is necessary," said his father. "It is good to pray at home but better to pray in God's house."

Obi thought: "What would happen if I stood up and said to him: 'Father, I no longer believe in your God'?" He knew it was impossible for him to do it, but he just wondered what would happen if he did. He often wondered like that. A few weeks ago in London he had wondered what would have happened if he had stood up and shouted to the smooth M.P. lecturing to African students on the Central African Federation: "Go away, you are all bloody hypocrites!" It was not quite the same thing, though. His father believed fervently in God; the smooth M.P. was just a bloody hypocrite.

"Did you have time to read your Bible while you were there?"

There was nothing for it but to tell a lie. Sometimes a lie was kinder than the truth. Obi knew why the question had been asked. He had read his verses so badly at prayers that evening.

"Sometimes," he replied, "but it was the Bible written in the English language."

"Yes," said his father. "I see."

There was a long pause in which Obi remembered with shame how he had stumbled through his portions as a child. In the first verse he had pronounced *ugwu* as *mountain* when it should be *circumcision*. Four or five voices had promptly corrected him, the first to register being his youngest sister, Eunice, who was eleven and in Standard Four.

The whole family sat round the enormous parlor table with the ancient hurricane lamp in the center. There were nine people in all—father, brother, six sisters, and Obi. When his father called out the portion for the day from the Scripture Union Card, Obi had impressed himself by finding it without difficulty in the Bible which he shared with Eunice. Prayers were then said for the opening of the eyes, and the reading began, each person reading one verse in turn.

Obi's mother sat in the background on a low stool. The four little children of her married daughters lay on the mat by her stool. She could read, but she never took part in the family reading. She merely listened to her husband and children. It had always been like that as far as the children could remember. She was a very devout woman, but Obi used to wonder whether, left to herself, she would not have preferred telling her children the folk stories that her mother had told her. In fact, she used to tell her eldest daughters stories. But that was before Obi was born. She stopped because her husband forbade her to do so.

"We are not heathens," he had said. "Stories like that are not for the people of the Church."

And Hannah had stopped telling her children folk stories. She was loyal to her husband and to her new faith. Her mother had joined the Church with her children after her husband's death. Hannah had already grown up when they ceased to be "people of nothing" and joined the "people of the Church." Such was the confidence of the early Christians that they called the others "the people of nothing" or sometimes, when they felt more charitable, "the people of the world."

Isaac Okonkwo was not merely a Christian; he was a catechist. In their first years of married life he made Hannah see the grave responsibility she carried as a catechist's wife. And as soon as she knew what was expected of her she did it, sometimes showing more zeal than even her husband. She taught her children not to accept food in neighbors' houses because she said they offered their food to idols. That fact alone set her children apart from all others for, among the Ibo, children were free to eat where they liked. One day a neighbor offered a piece of yam to Obi, who was then four years old. He shook his head like his older and wiser sisters, and then said: "We don't eat heathen food." His sister Janet tried too late to cover his mouth with her hand.

But there were occasional setbacks in this crusade. A year or two later when Obi had begun to go to school, such a setback did take place. There was one lesson which he loved and feared. It was called "Oral." During this period the teacher called on any pupil to tell the class a folk story. Obi loved these stories but he knew none which he could tell. One day the teacher called on him to face the class and tell them a story. As he came out and stood before them he trembled.

"*Olulu ofu oge*," he began in the tradition of folk tales, but that was all he knew. His lips quivered but no other sounds came out. The class burst into derisive laughter, and tears filled his eyes and rolled down his cheeks as he went back to his place.

As soon as he got home he told his mother about it. She told him to be patient until his father went to the evening prayer meeting.

Some weeks later Obi was called up again. He faced the class boldly and told one of the new stories his mother had told him. He even added a little touch to the end which made everyone laugh. It was the story of the wicked leopardess who wanted to eat the young lambs of his old friend the sheep. She went to the sheep's hut when she knew she had gone to market and began to search for the young lambs. She did not know that their mother had hidden them inside some of the palm-kernels lying around. At last she gave up the search and brought two stones to crack some of the kernels and eat before going, because she was very, very hungry. As soon as she cracked the first, the nut flew into the bush. She was amazed. The second also flew into the bush. And the third and eldest not only flew into the bush but, in Obi's version, slapped the leopardess in the eyes before doing so.

"You say you have only four days to stay with us?"

"Yes," said Obi. "But I will do my best to come again within a year. I must be in Lagos to see about getting a job."

"Yes," said his father slowly. "A job is the first thing. A person who has not secured a place on the floor should not begin to look for a mat." After a pause he said: "There are many things to talk about, but not tonight. You are tired and need sleep."

"I am not very tired, Father. But perhaps it is better to talk tomorrow. There is one thing, however, about which you should have a restful mind. There will be no question of John not finishing his course at the Grammar School."

"Good night, my son, and God bless you."

"Good night, Father."

He borrowed the ancient hurricane lamp to see his way to his room and bed. There was a brand-new white sheet on the old wooden bed with its hard grass-filled mattress. The pillow slips with their delicate floral designs were no doubt Esther's work. "Good old Esther!" Obi thought. He remembered when he was a little boy and Esther had just become a teacher. Everyone said that she should no longer be called Esther because it was disrespectful, but Miss. So she was called Miss. Sometimes Obi forgot and called her Esther, whereupon Charity told him how rude he was.

In those days Obi got on very well with his three eldest sisters, Esther, Janet, and Agnes, but not with Charity, who was his immediate elder. Charity's Ibo name was a "A girl is also good," but whenever they quarreled Obi called her "A girl is not good." Then she would beat him until he cried unless their mother happened to be around, in which case Charity would postpone the beating. She was as strong as iron and was feared by other children in the neighborhood, even the boys.

Obi did not sleep for a long time after he had lain down. He thought about his responsibilities. It was clear that his parents could no longer stand on their own. They had never relied on his father's meager pension. He planted yams and his wife planted cassava and coco yams. She also made soap from leachings of palm ash and oil and sold it to the villagers for a little profit. But now they were too old for these things.

"I must give them a monthly allowance from my salary." How much? Could he afford ten pounds? If only he did not have to pay back twenty pounds a month to the Umuofia Progressive Union. Then there was John's school fees.

"We'll manage somehow," he said aloud to himself. "One cannot have it both ways. There are many young men in this country today who would sacrifice themselves to get the opportunity I have had."

Outside a strong wind had suddenly arisen and the disturbed trees became noisy. Flashes of lightning showed through the jalousie. It was going to rain. Obi liked rain at night. He forgot his responsibilities and thought about Clara, how heavenly it would be on such a night to feel her cool body against his—the shapely thighs and the succulent breasts.

Why had she said he should not tell his parents about her yet? Could it be that her mind was still not made up? He would have liked to tell his mother at least. He knew she would be overjoyed. She once said she would be ready to depart when she had seen his first child. That was before he went to England; it must have been when Esther's first child was born. She now had three, Janet two, Agnes one. Agnes would have had two if her first child had lived. It must be dreadful to lose one's first child, especially for a little girl like Agnes; she was no more than a little girl really at the time she got married— in her behavior at least. Even now, she still had not quite grown up. Her mother always told her so. Obi smiled in the darkness as he remembered the little incident after prayers an hour or two ago.

Agnes had been asked to carry the little children, who were already asleep on the floor, to their beds.

"Wake them up to urinate first or they will do it in their beds," said Esther.

Agnes grabbed the first child by the wrist and pulled him up.

"Agnes! Agnes!" screamed their mother, who was sitting on a low stool beside the sleeping children, "I have always said that your head is not correct. How often must I tell you to call a child by name before waking him up?"

"Don't you know," Obi took up, pretending great anger, "that if you pull him up suddenly his soul may not be able to get back to his body before he wakes?"

The girls laughed. Obi had not changed a bit. He enjoyed teasing them, their mother not excepted. She smiled.

"You may laugh if laughter catches you," she said indulgently. "It does not catch me."

"That is why Father calls them the foolish virgins," said Obi.

It was now beginning to rain with thunder and lightning. At first large raindrops drummed on the iron roof. It was as though thousands of pebbles, each wrapped separately in a piece of cloth to break its fall, had been let loose from the sky. Obi wished that it was daytime so that he could see a tropical rain once more. It was now gathering strength. The drumming of large single drops gave way to a steady downpour.

"I had forgotten it could rain so heavily in November," he thought as he rearranged his loincloth to cover his whole body. Actually such rain was unusual. It was as though the deity presiding over the waters in the sky found, on checking his stock and counting off the months on his fingers, that there was too much rain left and that he had to do something drastic about it before the impending dry season.

Obi composed himself and went off to sleep.

CHAPTER SEVEN

OBI'S FIRST DAY IN THE CIVIL SERVICE WAS MEMORABLE, almost as memorable as his first day at the bush mission school in Umuofia nearly twenty years before. In those days white men were very rare. In fact, Mr. Jones had been the second white man Obi had set eyes on, and he had been nearly seven then. The first white man had been the Bishop of the Niger.

Mr. Jones was the Inspector of Schools and was feared throughout the province. It was said that he had fought during the Kaiser's war and that it had gone to his head. He was a huge man, over six feet tall. He rode a motorcycle which he always left about half a mile away so that he could enter a school unannounced. Then he was sure to catch somebody committing an offense. He visited a school about once in two years and he always did something which was remembered until his next visit. Two years before, he had thrown a boy out of a window. Now it was the headmaster who got into trouble. Obi never discovered what the trouble was because it had all been done in English. Mr. Jones was red with fury as he paced up and down, taking such ample strides that at one point Obi thought he was making straight for him. The headmaster, Mr. Nduka, was all the while trying to explain something.

"Shut up!" roared Mr. Jones, and followed it up with a slap. Simeon Nduka was one of those people who had taken to the ways of the white man rather late in life. And one of the things he had learnt in his youth was the great art of wrestling. In the twinkling of an eye Mr. Jones was flat on the floor and the school was thrown into confusion. Without knowing why, teachers and pupils all took to their heels. To throw a white man was like unmasking an ancestral spirit.

That was twenty years ago. Today few white men would dream of slapping a headmaster in his school and none at all would actually do it. Which is the tragedy of men like William Green, Obi's boss.

Obi had already met Mr. Green that morning. As soon as he had arrived he had been taken in to be introduced to him. Without rising from his seat or offering his hand Mr. Green muttered something to the effect that Obi would enjoy his work; one, if he wasn't bone-lazy, and two, if he was prepared to use his loaf. "I'm assuming you have one to use," he concluded.

A few hours later he appeared in Mr. Omo's office, where Obi had been posted for the day. Mr. Omo was the Administrative Assistant. He had put nearly thirty years' service into thousands of files, and would retire, or so he said, when his son had completed his legal studies in England. Obi was spending his first day in Mr. Omo's office to learn a few things about office administration.

Mr. Omo jumped to his feet as soon as Mr. Green came in. Simultaneously he pocketed the other half of the kola nut he was eating.

"Why hasn't the Study Leave file been passed to me?" Mr. Green asked.

"I thought . . ."

"You are not paid to think, Mr. Omo, but to do what

you are told. Is that clear? Now send the file to me immediately."

"Yes, sir."

Mr. Green slammed the door behind him and Mr. Omo carried the file personally to him. When he returned he began to rebuke a junior clerk who, it seemed, had caused all the trouble.

Obi had now firmly decided that he did not like Mr. Green and that Mr. Omo was one of his old Africans. As if to confirm his opinion the telephone rang. Mr. Omo hesitated, as he always did when the telephone rang, and then took it up as if it was liable to bite.

"Hello. Yes, sir." He handed it over to Obi with obvious relief. "Mr. Okonkwo, for you."

Obi took the telephone. Mr. Green wanted to know whether he had received a formal offer of appointment. Obi said, no, he hadn't.

"You say *sir* to your superior officers, Mr. Okonkwo," and the telephone was dropped with a deafening bang.

Obi bought a Morris Oxford a week after he received his letter of appointment. Mr. Green gave him a letter to the dealers saying that he was a senior civil servant entitled to a car advance. Nothing more was required. He walked into the shop and got a brand-new car.

Earlier on the same day Mr. Omo had sent for him to sign certain documents.

"Where is your stamp?" he asked as soon as Obi arrived.

"What stamp?" asked Obi.

"You get B.A. but you no know say you have to affix stamp to agreement?"

"What agreement?" asked Obi perplexed.

Mr. Omo laughed a laugh of derision. He had very bad teeth blackened by cigarettes and kola nuts. One was missing in front, and when he laughed the gap looked like a vacant plot in a slum. His junior clerks laughed with him out of loyalty.

"You think Government give you sixty pounds without signing agreement?"

It was only then that Obi understood what it was all about. He was to receive sixty pounds outfit allowance.

"This is a wonderful day," he told Clara on the telephone. "I have sixty pounds in my pocket, and I'm getting my car at two o'clock."

Clara screamed with delight. "Shall I ring Sam and tell him not to bother to send his car this evening?"

The Hon. Sam Okoli, Minister of State, had asked them to drinks and had offered to send his driver to fetch them. Clara lived in Yaba with her first cousin. She had been offered a job as Assistant Nursing Sister, and she would start work in a week or so. Then she would find more suitable lodgings. Obi still shared Joseph's room in Obalende but would move to a senior service flat in Ikoyi at the end of the week.

Obi was disposed to like the Hon. Sam Okoli from the moment he learnt that he had no designs on Clara. In fact he was getting married shortly to Clara's best friend and Clara had been asked to be chief bridesmaid.

"Come in, Clara. Come in, Obi," he said as if he had known both of them all his life. "That is a lovely car. How is it behaving? Come right in. You are looking very sweet, Clara. We haven't met, Obi, but I know all about you. I'm happy you are getting married to Clara. Sit down. Anywhere. And tell me what you will drink. Lady first; that is what the white man has brought. I respect the white man although we want them to go. Squash? God forbid! Nobody drinks squash in my house. Samson, bring sherry for Miss."

"Yes, sah," said Samson in immaculate white and brass buttons.

"Beer? Why not try a little whisky?"

"I don't touch spirits," said Obi.

"Many young people from overseas start that way," said Sam Okoli. "O.K., Samson, one beer, whisky and soda for me."

Obi looked round the luxurious sitting room. He had read the controversy in the Press when the Government had decided to build these ministers' houses at a cost of thirty-five thousand each.

"A very good house this," he said.

"It's not too bad," said the Minister.

"What an enormous radiogram!" Obi rose from his seat to go and have a closer look.

"It has a recording machine as well," explained the owner. As if he knew what Obi was thinking, he added: "It was not part of the house. I paid two-seventy-five pounds for it." He walked across the room and switched on the tape recorder.

"How do you like your work on the Scholarship Board? If you press this thing down, it begins to record. If you want to stop, you press this one. This is for playing records and this one is the radio. If I had a vacancy in my Ministry, I would have liked you to come and work there." He stopped the tape recorder, wound back, and then pressed the playback knob. "You will hear all our conversation, everything." He smiled with satisfaction as he listened to his own voice, adding an occasional commentary in pidgin.

"White man don go far. We just de shout for nothing," he said. Then he seemed to realize his position. "All the same they must go. This no be them country." He helped himself to another whisky, switched on the radio, and sat down.

"Do you have just one Assistant Secretary in your Ministry?" asked Obi.

"Yes, at present. I hope to get another one in April. I used to have a Nigerian as my A.S., but he was an idiot. His head was swollen like a soldier ant because he went to

Ibadan University. Now I have a white man who went to Oxford and he says 'sir' to me. Our people have a long way to go."

Obi sat with Clara in the back while the driver he had engaged that morning at four pounds ten a month drove them to Ikeja, twelve miles away, to have a special dinner in honor of the new car. But neither the drive nor the dinner was a great success. It was quite clear that Clara was not happy. Obi tried in vain to make her talk or relax.

"What's the matter?"

"Nothing. I'm just depressed, that's all."

It had been dark in the car. He put an arm round her and pulled her towards him.

"Not here, please."

Obi was hurt, especially as he knew his driver had heard.

"I'm sorry, dear," said Clara, putting her hand in his. "I will explain later."

"When?" Obi was alarmed by her tone.

"Today. After you have eaten."

"What do you mean? Aren't you eating?"

She said she did not feel like eating. Obi said in that case he too wouldn't eat. So they decided to eat. But when the food came they merely looked at it, even Obi, who had set out with a roaring appetite.

There was a film show which Clara suggested they should see. Obi said no, he wanted to find out what was on her mind. They went for a walk in the direction of the swimming pool.

Until Obi met Clara on board the cargo boat *Sasa* he had thought of love as another grossly overrated European invention. It was not that he was indifferent to women. On the contrary, he had been quite intimate with a few in England—a Nigerian, a West Indian, English girls, and so on. But these intimacies which Obi regarded as love were neither deep nor sincere. There was always a part of him, the thinking part, which seemed to stand outside it all watching the passionate embrace with cynical disdain. The result was that one half of Obi might kiss a girl and murmur: "I love you," but the other half would say: "Don't be silly." And it was always this second half that triumphed in the end when the glamor had evaporated with the heat, leaving a ridiculous anticlimax.

With Clara it was different. It had been from the very first. There was never a superior half at Obi's elbow wearing a patronizing smile.

"I can't marry you," she said suddenly as Obi tried to kiss her under the tall frangipani tree at the edge of the swimming pool, and exploded into tears.

"I don't understand you, Clara." And he really didn't. Was this woman's game to bind him more firmly? But Clara was not like that; she had no coyness in her. Not much, anyway. That was one of the things Obi liked best about her. She had seemed so sure of herself that, unlike other women, she did not consider how quickly or cheaply she was captured.

"Why can't you marry me?" He succeeded in sounding unruffled. For answer she threw herself at him and began to weep violently on his shoulder.

"What's the matter, Clara? Tell me." He was no longer unruffled. There was a hint of tears in his voice.

"I am an *osu,*" she wept. Silence. She stopped weeping and quietly disengaged herself from him. Still he said nothing.

"So you see we cannot get married," she said, quite firmly, almost gaily—a terrible kind of gaiety. Only the tears showed she had wept.

"Nonsense!" said Obi. He shouted it almost, as if by shouting it now he could wipe away those seconds of silence, when everything had seemed to stop, waiting in vain for him to speak.

Joseph was asleep when he got back. It was past midnight. The door was shut but not locked, and he walked in quietly. But the slight whining of the door was enough to wake Joseph. Without waiting to undress, Obi told him the story.

"The very thing I was thinking to ask you. I was thinking how such a good and beautiful girl could remain unmarried until now." Obi was undressing absentmindedly. "Anyhow, you are lucky to know at the beginning. No harm is done yet. The eye is not harmed by sleep," Joseph said somewhat pointlessly. He noticed that Obi was not paying any attention.

"I am going to marry her," Obi said.

"What!" Joseph sat up in bed.

"I am going to marry her."

"Look at me," said Joseph, getting up and tying his coverlet as a loincloth. He now spoke in English. "You know book, but this is no matter for book. Do you know what an *osu* is? But how can you know?" In that short question he said in effect that Obi's mission-house upbringing and European education had made him a stranger in his country—the most painful thing one could say to Obi.

"I know more about it than yourself," he said, "and I'm going to marry the girl. I wasn't actually seeking your approval."

Joseph thought the best thing was to drop the matter for the present. He went back to bed and was soon snoring.

Obi felt better and more confident in his decision now that there was an opponent, the first of hundreds to come, no doubt. Perhaps it was not a decision really; for him there could be only one choice. It was scandalous that in the middle of the twentieth century a man could be barred from marrying a girl simply because her great-great-great-great-grandfather had been dedicated to serve a god, thereby setting himself apart and turning his descendants into a forbidden caste to the end of Time. Quite unbelievable. And here was an educated man telling Obi he did not understand. "Not even my mother can stop me," he said as he lay down beside Joseph.

At half-past two on the following day he called for Clara and told her they were going to Kingsway to buy an engagement ring.

"When?" was all she could ask.

"Now, now."

"But I haven't said I . . ."

"Oh, don't waste my time. I have other things to do. I haven't got my steward yet, and I haven't bought my pots and pans."

"Yes, of course, it is tomorrow you are moving into your flat. I'm almost forgetting."

They went in the car and made for the jeweler's shop in Kingsway and bought a twenty-pound ring. Obi's heavy wad of sixty pounds was now very much reduced. Thirty something pounds. Nearly forty.

"What about a Bible?" Clara asked.

"What Bible?"

"To go with the ring. Don't you know that?"

Obi didn't know that. They went over to the C.M.S. Bookshop and paid for a handsome little Bible with a zip.

"Everything has a zip these days," said Obi, looking instinctively at his trouser front to make sure he had not forgotten to do the zip up, as had happened on one or two occasions.

They spent the whole afternoon shopping. At first Obi was as interested as Clara in the different utensils she was buying for him. But after an hour in which only one little saucepan had been bagged he lost any semblance of interest in the proceedings and simply trudged behind Clara like an obedient dog. She would reject an aluminum pot in one shop, and walk the whole length of Broad Street to another to buy the very same thing at the very same price.

"What is the difference between this one and the one we saw at U.T.C.?"

"Men are blind," she said.

When Obi got back to Joseph's room it was nearly eleven o'clock. Joseph was still up. In fact he had been waiting all the afternoon to complete the discussion they had suspended last night.

"How is Clara?" he asked. He succeeded in making it sound casual and unrehearsed. Obi was not prepared to plunge headlong into it. He wanted to begin at the fringes as he used to do many years ago when he was confronted with a morning bath in the cold harmattan season. Of all the parts of his body, his back liked cold water the least. He would stand before the bucket of water thinking how best to tackle it. His mother would call: "Obi, haven't you finished? You will be late for school and they will flog you." He would then stir the water with one finger. After that he would wash his feet, then his legs up to the knees, then the arm up to the elbow, then the rest of his arms and legs, the face and head, the belly, and finally, accompanied by a leap into the air, his back. He wanted to adopt the same method now.

"She is fine," he said. "Your Nigerian police are very cheeky, you know."

"They are useless," said Joseph, not wanting to discuss the police.

"I asked the driver to take us to the Victoria Beach Road. When we got there it was so cold that Clara refused to leave her seat. So we stayed at the back of the car, talking."

"Where was the driver?" asked Joseph.

"He walked a little distance away to gaze at the lighthouse. Anyway, we were not there ten minutes before a police car drew up beside us and one of them flashed his torch. He said: 'Good evening, sir.' I said: 'Good evening.' Then he said: 'Is she your wife?' I remained very cool and said: 'No.' Then he said: 'Where you pick am?' I couldn't stand that, so I blew up. Clara told me in Ibo to call the driver and go away. The policeman immediately changed. He was Ibo, you see. He said he didn't know we were Ibos. He said many people these days were fond of taking other men's wives to the beach. Just think of that. *'Where you pick am?'* "

"What did you do after that?"

"We came away. We couldn't possibly stay after that. By the way, we are now engaged. I gave her a ring this afternoon."

"Very good," said Joseph bitterly. He thought for a while and then asked: "Are you going to marry the English way or are you going to ask your people to approach her people according to custom?"

"I don't know yet. It depends on what my father says."

"Did you tell him about it during your visit?"

"No, because I hadn't decided then."

"He will not agree to it," said Joseph. "Tell anyone that I said so."

"I can handle them," said Obi, "especially my mother."

"Look at me, Obi." Joseph invariably asked people to look at him. "What you are going to do concerns not only yourself but your whole family and future generations. If one finger brings oil it soils the others. In future, when we are all civilized, anybody may marry anybody. But that time has not come. We of this generation are only pioneers."

"What is a pioneer? Someone who shows the way. That is what I am doing. Anyway, it is too late to change now."

"It is not," said Joseph. "What is an engagement ring? Our fathers did not marry with rings. It is not too late to change. Remember you are the one and only Umuofia son to be educated overseas. We do not want to be like the unfortunate child who grows his first tooth and grows a decayed one. What sort of encouragement will your action give to the poor men and women who collected the money?"

Obi was getting a little angry. "It was only a loan, remember. I shall pay it all back to the last anini."

Obi knew better than anyone else that his family would violently oppose the idea of marrying an *osu*. Who wouldn't? But for him it was either Clara or nobody. Family ties were all very well as long as they did not interfere with Clara. "If I could convince my mother," he thought, "all would be well."

There was a special bond between Obi and his mother. Of all her eight children Obi was nearest her heart. Her neighbors used to call her "Janet's mother" until Obi was born, and then she immediately became "Obi's mother." Neighbors have an unfailing instinct in such matters. As a child Obi took this special relationship very much for granted. But when he was about ten something happened which gave it concrete form in his young mind. He had a rusty razorblade with which he sharpened his pencil or sometimes cut up a grasshopper. One day he forgot this implement in his pocket and it cut his mother's hand very badly when she was washing his clothes on a stone in the stream. She returned with the clothes unwashed and her hand dripping with blood. For some reason or other, whenever Obi thought affectionately of his mother, his mind went back to that shedding of her blood. It bound him very firmly to her.

When he said to himself: "If I could convince my mother," he was almost certain that he could.

CHAPTER EIGHT

THE UMUOFIA PROGRESSIVE UNION, LAGOS BRANCH, HELD its meetings on the first Saturday of every month. Obi did not attend the November meeting because he was visiting Umuofia at the time. His friend Joseph made his excuses.

The next meeting took place on 1 December 1956. Obi remembered that date because it was important in his life. Joseph had telephoned him in the office to remind him that the meeting began at 4.30 P.M. "You will not forget to call for me?" he asked.

"Of course not," said Obi. "Expect me at four."

"Good! See you later." Joseph always put on an impressive manner when speaking on the telephone. He never spoke Ibo or pidgin English at such moments. When he hung up he told his colleagues: "That na my brother. Just return from overseas. B.A. (Honors) Classics." He always preferred the fiction of Classics to the truth of English. It sounded more impressive.

"What department he de work?"

"Secretary to the Scholarship Board."

" 'E go make plenty money there. Every student who wan' go England go de see am for house."

" 'E no be like dat," said Joseph. "Him na gentleman. No fit take bribe."

"Na so," said the other in unbelief.

At four fifteen Obi arrived at Joseph's in his new Morris Oxford. That was one reason why Joseph had looked forward to this particular meeting. He was going to share

77

in the glory of the car. It was going to be a great occasion
for the Umuofia Progressive Union when one of their sons
arrived at their meeting in a pleasure car. Joseph as a very
close friend of Obi would reflect some of the glory. He
was impeccably turned out for the occasion: gray flannel
trousers, white nylon shirt, spotted dark tie, and black
shoes. Although he did not say it, he was disappointed at
Obi's casual appearance. It was true he wanted to share in
the glory of the car, but he did not care to be called the
outsider who wept louder than the bereaved. It was not
beyond Umuofia men to make such embarrassing com-
ments.

The reaction of the meeting was better than even
Joseph expected. Although Obi had arrived at his place at
four fifteen Joseph had delayed their departure until five
when he knew the meeting would be full. The fine for
lateness was one penny, but what was that beside the glory
of stepping out of a pleasure car in the full gaze of
Umuofia? As it turned out, nobody thought of the fine.
They clapped and cheered and danced when they saw the
car pull up.

"*Umuofia kwenu!*" shouted one old man.

"Ya!" replied everyone in unison.

"*Umuofia kwenu!*"

"Ya!"

"*Kwenu!*"

"Ya!"

"*Ife awolu Ogoli azua n'afia,*" he said.

Obi was given a seat beside the President and had to
answer innumerable questions about his job and about his
car before the meeting settled down again to business.

Joshua Udo, a messenger in the Post Office, had been
sacked for sleeping while on duty. According to him, he
had not been sleeping but thinking. But the Chief Clerk
had been looking for a way to deal with him since he had
not completed the payment of ten pounds' bribe which he
had promised when he was employed. Joshua was now

asking his countrymen to "borrow" him ten pounds to look for another job.

The meeting had practically agreed to this when it was disturbed by Obi's arrival. The President was just giving Joshua a piece of his mind on the subject of sleeping in the office, as a preliminary to lending him public funds.

"You did not leave Umuofia four hundred miles away to come and sleep in Lagos," he told him. "There are enough beds in Umuofia. If you don't want to work, you should return there. You messengers are all like that. I have one in my office who is always getting permission to go to the latrine. Anyway, I move that we approve a loan of ten pounds to Mr. Joshua Udo for the ... er ... er the explicit purpose of seeking reengagement." The last sentence was said in English because of its legal nature. The loan was approved. Then by way of light relief someone took up the President on his statement that it was work that brought them four hundred miles to Lagos.

"It is money, not work," said the man. "We left plenty of work at home. ... Anyone who likes work can return home, take up his matchet and go into that bad bush between Umuofia and Mbaino. It will keep him occupied to his last days." The meeting agreed that it was money, not work, that brought them to Lagos.

"Let joking pass," said the old man who had earlier on greeted Umuofia in warlike salute. "Joshua is now without a job. We have given him ten pounds. But ten pounds does not talk. If you stand a hundred pounds here where I stand now, it will not talk. That is why we say that he who has people is richer than he who has money. Everyone of us here should look out for openings in his department and put in a word for Joshua." This was greeted with approval.

"Thanks to the Man Above," he continued, "we now have one of our sons in the senior service. We are not going to ask him to bring his salary to share among us. It is in little things like this that he can help us. It is our fault if we do not approach him. Shall we kill a snake and carry it in our hand when we have a bag for putting long things in?" He took his seat.

"Your words are very good," said the President. "We have the same thought in our minds. But we must give the young man time to look round first and know what is what."

The meeting supported the President by their murmurs. "Give the young man time." "Let him settle down." Obi felt very uneasy. But he knew they meant well. Perhaps it would not be too difficult to manage them.

The next item on the agenda was a motion of censure on the President and executive for mishandling Obi's reception. Obi was amazed. He had thought that his reception went very well. But not so the three young men who sponsored the motion. Nor, as it turned out, a dozen or so other young people. Their complaint was that they were not given any of the two dozen bottles of beer which had been bought. The top people and elders had monopolized it, leaving the young people with two kegs of sour palm-wine. As everyone knew, Lagos palm-wine was really no palm-wine at all but water—an infinite dilution.

This accusation caused a lively exchange of hard words for the better part of an hour. The President called the young men "ungrateful ingrates whose stock-in-trade was character-assassination." One of the young people suggested that it was immoral to use public funds to buy beer for one's private thirst. The words were hard, but Obi felt somehow that they lacked bitterness; especially since they were English words taken straight from today's newspaper. When it was all over the President announced that their honored son Obi Okonkwo had a few words to say to them. This announcement was received with great joy.

Obi rose to his feet and thanked them for having such a useful meeting, for did not the Psalmist say that it was good for brethren to meet together in harmony? "Our fathers also have a saying about the danger of living apart. They say it is the curse of the snake. If all snakes lived together in one place, who would approach them? But they live every one unto himself and so fall easy prey to man." Obi knew he was making a good impression. His listeners nodded their heads and made suitable rejoinders. Of course it was all a prepared speech, but it did not sound overrehearsed.

He spoke about the wonderful welcome they had given him on his return. "If a man returns from a long journey and no one says *ndo* to him he feels like one who has not arrived." He tried to improvise a joke about beer and palm-wine, but it did not come off, and he hurried to the next point. He thanked them for the sacrifices they had made to send him to England. He would try his best to justify their confidence. The speech which had started off one hundred percent in Ibo was now fifty-fifty. But his audience still seemed highly impressed. They liked good Ibo, but they also admired English. At last he got round to his main subject. "I have one little request to place before you. As you all know, it takes a little time to settle down again after an absence of four years. I have many little private matters to settle. My request is this, that you give me four months before I start to pay back my loan."

"That is a small matter," said someone. "Four months is a short time. A debt may get moldy, but it never decays."

Yes, it was a small matter. But it was clear that not everyone thought so. Obi even heard someone ask what he was going to do with the big money which Government would give him.

"Your words are very good," said the President at length. "I do not think anyone here will say no to your request. We will give you four months. Do I speak for Umuofia?"

"Ya!" they replied.

"But there are two words I should like to drop before you. You are very young, a child of yesterday. You know book. But book stands by itself and experience stands by itself. So I am not afraid to talk to you."

Obi's heart began to pound heavily.

"You are one of us, so we must bare our minds to you. I have lived in this Lagos for fifteen years. I came here on August the sixth, nineteen hundred and forty-one. Lagos is a bad place for a young man. If you follow its sweetness, you will perish. Perhaps you will ask why I am saying all this. I know what Government pays senior service people. What you get in one month is what some of your brothers here get in one year. I have already said that we will give you four months. We can even give you one year. But are we doing you any good?"

A big lump caught in Obi's throat.

"What the Government pays you is more than enough unless you go into bad ways." Many of the people said: "God forbid!" "We cannot afford bad ways," went on the President. "We are pioneers building up our families and our town. And those who build must deny ourselves many pleasures. We must not drink because we see our neighbors drink or run after women because our thing stands up. You may ask why I am saying all this, I have heard that you are moving around with a girl of doubtful ancestry, and even thinking of marrying her. . . ."

Obi leapt to his feet trembling with rage. At such times words always deserted him.

"Please sit down, Mr. Okonkwo," said the President calmly.

"Sit down, my foot!" Obi shouted in English. "This is preposterous! I could take you to court for that . . . for that . . . for that. . . ."

"You may take me to court when I have finished."

"I am not going to listen to you anymore. I take back my request. I shall start paying you back at the end of this month. Now, this minute! But don't you dare interfere in my affairs again. And if this is what you meet about," he said in Ibo, "you may cut off my two legs if you ever find

em here again." He made for the door. A number of
eople tried to intercept him. "Please sit down." "Cool
own." "There is no quarrel." Everybody was talking at
nce. Obi pushed his way through and made blindly for
is car with half a dozen people at his heels pleading that
e return.

"Drive off!" he screamed at the driver as soon as he
ot into the car.

"Obi, please," said Joseph, miserably leaning on the
indow.

"Get out!"

The car drove off. Halfway to Ikoyi he ordered the
river to stop and go back to Lagos, to Clara's lodgings.

CHAPTER NINE

HE PROSPECT OF WORKING WITH MR. GREEN AND MR.
mo did not particularly appeal to Obi, but he soon found
at it was not as bad as he had thought. For one thing he
as given a separate office, which he shared with Mr.
reen's attractive English secretary. He saw very little of
Ir. Omo and only saw Mr. Green when he rushed in to
ark orders at him or at Miss Marie Tomlinson.

"Isn't he odd?" said Miss Tomlinson on one occasion.
But he's really not a bad man."

"Of course not," replied Obi. He knew that many of
ese secretaries were planted to spy on Africans. One of
eir tactics was to pretend to be very friendly and broad-
inded. One had to watch what one said. Not that he
ared whether or not Mr. Green knew what he thought of

his type. In fact, he ought to know. But he was not going to get it through an *agent provocateur*.

As the weeks passed, however, Obi's guard began to come down "small small," as they say. It started with Clara's visit to his office one morning to tell him something or other. Miss Tomlinson had heard her voice on the telephone a few times and had commented on its attractiveness. Obi introduced them, and was a little surprised at the English woman's genuine delight. When Clara left she talked about nothing else for the rest of the day. "Isn't she beautiful? Aren't you lucky? When are you getting married? I shouldn't wait if I were you," and so on and so forth.

Obi felt like a clumsy schoolboy earning his first praise for doing something extraordinarily clever. He began to see Miss Tomlinson in a different light. If it was part of her tactics, it was really a very clever one for which she deserved credit. But it did not look clever or forced. It seemed to have come straight from her heart.

The telephone rang and Miss Tomlinson answered it.

"Mr. Okonkwo? Right. Hold on for him. For you, Mr. Okonkwo."

Obi's telephone was in parallel with hers. He thought it was Clara, but it was only the receptionist downstairs.

"A gentleman? Send him up, please. He want speak to me there? All right, I de come down. Now now."

The gentleman was in a three-piece suit and carried a rolled umbrella. Obviously a new arrival from England.

"Good morning. My name is Okonkwo."

"Mark is mine. How do you do?"

They shook hands.

"I've come to consult you about something— semiofficial and semiprivate."

"Let's go up to my office, shall we?"

"Thank you very much."

Obi led the way.

"You have just come back to Nigeria?" he asked as they mounted the stairs.

"I've been back now six months."

"I see." He opened the door. "After you."

Mr. Mark stepped in, and then pulled up suddenly as if he had seen a snake across his path. But he recovered quickly enough and walked in.

"Good morning," he said to Miss Tomlinson, all smiles. Obi dragged another chair to his table and Mr. Mark sat down.

"And what can I do for you?"

To his amazement Mr. Mark replied in Ibo:

"If you don't mind, shall we talk in Ibo? I didn't know you had a European here."

"Just as you like. Actually I didn't think you were Ibo. What is your problem?" He tried to sound casual.

"Well, it is like this. I have a sister who has just passed her School Certificate in Grade One. She wants to apply for a Federal Scholarship to study in England."

Although he spoke in Ibo, there were some words that he had to say in English. Words like *school certificate* and *scholarship*. He lowered his voice to a whisper when he came to them.

"You want application forms?" asked Obi.

"No, no, no. I have got those. But it is like this. I was told that you are the secretary of the Scholarship Commission and I thought that I should see you. We are both Ibos and I cannot hide anything from you. It is all very well sending in forms, but you know what our country is. Unless you see people . . ."

"In this case it is not necessary to see anybody. The only . . ."

"I was actually thinking of coming round to your house, but the man who told me about you did not know where you lived."

"I'm sorry, Mr. Mark, but I really don't understand what you are driving at." He said this in English, much to

Mr. Mark's consternation. Miss Tomlinson pricked up her ears like a dog that is not quite sure whether someone has mentioned bones.

"I'm sorry—er—Mr. Okonkwo. But don't get me wrong. I know this is the wrong place to—er . . ."

"I don't think there is any point in continuing this discussion," Obi said again in English. "If you don't mind, I'm rather busy." He rose to his feet. Mr. Mark also rose, muttered a few apologies, and made for the door.

"He's forgotten his umbrella," remarked Miss Tomlinson as Obi returned to his seat.

"Oh, dear." He took the umbrella and rushed out.

Miss Tomlinson was eagerly waiting to hear what he would say when he came back, but he simply sat down as if nothing had happened and opened a file. He knew she was watching him, and he wrinkled his forehead in pretended concentration.

"That was short and sweet," she said.

"Oh, yes. He is a nuisance." He did not look up and the conversation lapsed.

Throughout that morning Obi felt strangely elated. It was not unlike the feeling he had some years ago in England after his first woman. She had said almost in so many words what she was coming for when she agreed to visit Obi in his lodgings. "I'll teach you how to dance the high-life when you come," he had said. "That would be grand," she replied eagerly, "and perhaps a little low life too." And she had smiled mischievously. When the day arrived Obi was scared. He had heard that it was possible to disappoint a woman. But he did not disappoint her, and when it was over he felt strangely elated. She said she thought she had been attacked by a tiger.

After his encounter with Mr. Mark he did feel like a tiger. He had won his first battle hands-down. Everyone said it was impossible to win. They said a man expects you to accept "kola" from him for services rendered, and until you do, his mind is never at rest. He feels like the inexperienced kite that carried away a duckling and was ordered by its mother to return it because the duck had said nothing, made no noise, just walked away. "There is some grave danger in that kind of silence. Go and get a chick. We know the hen. She shouts and curses, and the matter ends there." A man to whom you do a favor will not understand if you say nothing, make no noise, just walk away. You may cause more trouble by refusing a bribe than by accepting it. Had not a Minister of State said, albeit in an unguarded, alcoholic moment, that the trouble was not in receiving bribes, but in failing to do the thing for which the bribe was given? And if you refuse, how do you know that a "brother" or a "friend" is not receiving on your behalf, having told everyone that he is your agent? Stuff and nonsense! It was easy to keep one's hands clean. It required no more than the ability to say: "I'm sorry, Mr. So-and-So, but I cannot continue this discussion. Good morning." One should not, of course, be unduly arrogant. After all, the temptation was not really overwhelming. But in all modesty one could not say it had been nonexistent. Obi was finding it more and more impossible to live on what was left of his forty-seven pounds ten after he had paid twenty to the Umuofia Progressive Union and sent ten to his parents. Even now he had no idea where John's school fees for next term would come from. No, one could not say he had no need of money.

He had just finished his lunch of pounded yams and egusi soup and was sprawling on the sofa. The soup had been particularly well prepared—with meat and fresh fish —and he had overeaten. Whenever he ate too much pounded yam he felt like a boa that had swallowed a goat. He sprawled helplessly, waiting for some of it to digest, to give him room to breathe.

A car pulled up outside. He thought it was one of the five other occupants of the block of six flats. He knew none of them by name, and only some by sight. They were all Europeans. He spoke about once a month with one of them, the tall P.W.D. man who lived on the other side of the same floor. But his speaking to him had nothing to do with sharing the same floor. This man was in charge of the common garden and collected ten and sixpence every month from each occupant to pay the garden boy. So Obi knew him well by sight. He also knew one of those upstairs who regularly brought an African prostitute home on Saturday nights.

The car started again. It was clearly a taxi, for only taxi drivers could rev up their engines that way. There was a timid knock on Obi's door. Who could it be? Clara was on duty that afternoon. Joseph, perhaps. For months now he had been trying to regain the blissful seat in Obi's affections which he had lost at that ill-fated meeting of the Umuofia Progressive Union. His crime was that he had told the President in confidence of Obi's engagement to an outcast girl. He had pleaded for forgiveness: he had only told the President in confidence in the hope that he might use his position as the father of Umuofia people in Lagos to reason privately with Obi.

"Never mind," Obi had told him. "Let us forget about it." But he had not forgotten. He had stopped visiting Joseph in his lodgings. As for Clara, she did not want to set eyes on Joseph again. Obi was sometimes amazed and terrified at the intensity of her hate, knowing how much she had liked him before. Now he was slippery, he was envious, he was even capable of poisoning Obi. The incident, like a bath of palm-wine on incipient measles, had brought all the ugly rashes to the surface.

Obi opened the door with a very dark frown on his face. Instead of Joseph, there was a girl at the door.

"Good afternoon," he said, completely transformed.

"I am looking for Mr. Okonkwo," she said.

"Speaking. Come right in." He was surprised at his own sudden gaiety; the girl was, after all, a complete stranger, albeit a most attractive one. So he pulled in his horns.

"Please sit down. By the way, I don't think we've met before."

"No. I am Elsie Mark."

"Pleased to meet you, Miss Mark." She smiled a most delicious smile, showing a faultless set of immaculate teeth. There was a little gap between the two front ones, rather like Clara's. Someone had said that girls with that kind of teeth are very warm-blooded. He sat down. He wasn't shy as he usually was with girls, and yet he didn't know what to say next.

"You must be surprised at my visit." She was now speaking in Ibo.

"I didn't know you were Ibo." As soon as he said it light broke through. What was left of his gaiety vanished. The girl must have noticed a change in his expression or perhaps a movement of the hands. She avoided his eyes and her words came hesitantly. She was testing the slippery ground with one wary foot after another before committing her whole body.

"I'm sorry my brother came to your office. I told him not to."

"It's perfectly all right," Obi found himself saying. "I told him that—er—that with your Grade One certificate you stood a very good chance. It all depends on you really, how much you impress members of the Board at the interview."

"The most important thing," she said, "is to be sure that I am selected to appear before the Board."

"Yes. But as I said, you stand as good chance as anybody else."

"But people with Grade One are sometimes left out in favor of those with Grade Two or even Three."

"I've no doubt that may happen sometimes. But all other things being equal. . . . I'm sorry I haven't offered you anything. I'm a very bad host. Can I bring you a Coca-Cola?" She smiled shyly with her eyes. "Yes?" He rushed off to his refrigerator and brought out a bottle. He

took a long time opening it and pouring it into a glass. He
was thinking furiously.

She accepted the glass and smiled her thanks. She must
be about seventeen or eighteen. A mere girl, Obi thought.
And already so wise in the ways of the world. They sat in
silence for a long time.

"Last year," she said suddenly, "none of the girls in our
school who got Grade One was given a scholarship."

"Perhaps they did not impress the Board."

"It wasn't that. It was because they did not see the
members at home."

"So you intend to see the members?"

"Yes."

"Is a scholarship as important as all that? Why doesn't
a relation of yours pay for you to go to a university?"

"Our father spent all his money on our brother. He
went to read Medicine but failed his exams. He switched
over to Engineering and failed again. He was in England
for twelve years."

"Was that the man who came to see me today?" She
nodded. "What does he do for a living?"

"He is teaching in a Community Secondary School."
She was now looking very sad. "He returned at the end of
the last year because our father died and we had no more
money."

Obi felt very sorry for her. She was obviously an intelli-
gent girl who had set her mind, like so many other young
Nigerians, on university education. And who could blame
them? Certainly not Obi. It was rather sheer hypocrisy to
ask if a scholarship was as important as all that or if
university education was worth it. Every Nigerian knew
the answer. It was yes.

A university degree was the philosopher's stone. It
transmuted a third-class clerk on one hundred and fifty a
year into a senior civil servant on five hundred and seventy, with car and luxuriously furnished quarters at nominal
rent. And the disparity in salary and amenities did not tell

even half the story. To occupy a "European post" was second only to actually being a European. It raised a man from the masses to the élite whose small talk at cocktail parties was: "How's the car behaving?"

"Please, Mr. Okonkwo, you must help me. I'll do whatever you ask." She avoided his eyes. Her voice was a little unsteady, and Obi thought he saw a hint of tears in her eyes.

"I'm sorry, terribly sorry, but I don't see that I can make any promises."

Another car drew up outside with a screech of brakes, and Clara rushed in, as was her fashion, humming a popular song. She stopped abruptly on seeing the girl.

"Hello, Clara. This is Miss Mark."

"How do you do?" she said stiffly, with a slight nod of the head. She did not offer her hand. "How did you like the soup?" she asked Obi. "I'm afraid I prepared it in a hurry." In those two short sentences she sought to establish one or two facts for the benefit of the strange girl. First, by her sophisticated un-Nigerian accent she showed that she was a been-to. You could tell a been-to not only by her phonetics but by her walk—quick, short steps instead of the normal leisurely gait. In company of her less fortunate sisters she always found an excuse for saying: "When I was in England. . . ." Secondly, her propriety air seemed to tell the girl: "You had better try elsewhere."

"I thought you were on this afternoon."

"It was a mistake. I'm off today."

"Why did you have to go away then, after making the soup?"

"Oh, I had such a lot of washing to do. Aren't you offering me anything to drink? O.K., I'll serve myself."

"I'm terribly sorry, dear. Sit down. I'll get it for you."

"No. Too late." She went to the fridge and took out a bottle of ginger beer. "What's happened to the other ginger beer?" she asked. "There were two."

"I think you had one yesterday."

"Did I? Oh, yes, I remember." She came back and sank heavily into the sofa beside Obi. "Gosh, it's hot!"

"I think I must be going," said Miss Mark.

"I'm sorry I can't promise anything definite," said Obi, getting up. She did not answer, only smiled sadly.

"How are you getting back to town?"

"Perhaps I will see a taxi."

"I'll run you down to Tinubu Square. Taxis are very rare here. Come along, Clara, let's take her down to Tinubu."

"I'm sorry I came at such an awkward time," said Clara as they drove back to Ikoyi from Tinubu Square.

"Don't be ridiculous. What do you mean awkward time?"

"You thought I was on duty." She laughed. "I'm sorry about that. Who is she, anyway? I must say she is very good-looking. And I went and poured sand into your *garri*. I'm sorry, my dear."

Obi told her not to behave like a silly little girl. "I won't say another word to you if you don't shut up," he said.

"You needn't say anything if you don't want to. Shall we call and say hello to Sam?"

The Minister was not in when they got to his house. It appeared there was a Cabinet meeting.

"Wetin Master and Madam go drink?" asked his steward.

"Make you no worry, Samson. Just tell Minister say we call."

"You go return again?" asked Samson.

"Not today."

"You say you no go drink small sometin?"

"No, thank you. We go drink when we come again. Bye-bye."

When they got back to Obi's flat he said: "I had a very interesting experience today." And he told her of Mr.

Mark's visit to his office and gave her a detailed account of all that transpired between Miss Mark and himself before her arrival.

When he finished, Clara said nothing for a little while.

"Are you satisfied?" asked Obi.

"I think you were too severe on the man," she said.

"You think I should have encouraged him to talk about bribing me?"

"After all, offering money is not as bad as offering one's body. And yet you gave her a drink and a lift back to town." She laughed. "Na so this world be."

Obi wondered.

CHAPTER TEN

FOR ONE BRIEF MOMENT A YEAR AGO MR. GREEN HAD taken an interest in Obi's personal affairs—if one could call it taking an interest. Obi had just taken delivery of his new car.

"You will do well to remember," said Mr. Green, "that at this time every year you will be called upon to cough up forty pounds for your insurance." It was like the voice of Joel the son of Pethuel. "It is, of course, none of my business really. But in a country where even the educated have not reached the level of thinking about tomorrow, one has a clear duty." He made the word "educated" taste like vomit. Obi thanked him for his advice.

And now at last the day of the Lord had come. He spread the insurance renewal letter before him on the table. Forty-two pounds! He had just a little over thirteen

pounds in the bank. He folded the letter and put it into
one of his drawers where he had his personal bits and
pieces like postage stamps, receipts, and quarterly state-
ments from the bank. A letter in a semiliterate hand caught
his eye. He brought it out and read again.

Dear Sir,
   It is absolutely deplorable to me hence I have to beg
you respectfully to render me with help. At one side of it
looks shameful of my asking you for this help, but if only
I am sincere to myself, having the truth that I am wanting
because of the need, I wish you pardon me. My request
from you is 30/—(thirty shillings), assuring you of every
truth to do the refund prompt, on the payday, 26 November 1957.
   I wish the best of your consideration.
                              Yours obedient servant,
                                        Charles Ibe.

   Obi had forgotten all about it. No wonder Charles
flitted in and out of his office nowadays without stopping
to exchange greetings in Ibo. Charles was one of the
messengers in the department. Obi had asked him what
the great need was, and he said his wife had just given
birth to their fifth child. Obi, who happened to be carrying
about four pounds in his pocket, had lent him thirty
shillings straightaway and forgotten all about it—until
now. He sent for Charles and asked him in Ibo (so that
Miss Tomlinson would not understand) why he had not
fulfilled his promise. Charles scratched his head and
renewed his promise, this time for the end of December.
   "I shall find it difficult to trust you in future," Obi said
in English.
   "Ah, no, *Oga*, Master. E no be like dat I beg. I go pay
end of mont prompt." He then reverted to Ibo. "Our
people have a saying that a debt may become moldy but it

never rots. There are many people in this department, but I did not go to them. I came to you."

"That was very kind of you," said Obi, knowing full well that the point would be missed. It was.

"Yes, there are many people here, but I did not go to them. I take you as my special master. Our people have a saying that when there is a big tree small ones climb on its back to reach the sun. You are a small boy in years, but . . ."

"O.K., Charles. End of December. If you fail I shall report the matter to Mr. Green."

"Ah! I no go fail at all. If I fail my Oga, who I go go meet next time?"

And on that rhetorical note the matter rested for the moment. Obi looked at Charles's letter again and saw with wry amusement that in the original manuscript he had written: "My request from you is only 30/—(thirty shillings)"; he had then crossed out only, no doubt after mature deliberation.

He shoved the letter back in the drawer to spend the night with the insurance notice. There was nothing for it but to go to the bank manager tomorrow morning and ask for an overdraft of fifty pounds. He had been told that it was fairly easy for a senior civil servant, whose salary was paid into the bank, to obtain an overdraft of that order. Meanwhile there was little point in thinking about it anymore. Charles's attitude was undoubtedly the healthiest in these circumstances. If one didn't laugh, one would have to cry. It seemed that was the way Nigeria was built.

But no amount of philosophy could take his mind right off that notice. "No one can say I have been extravagant. If I had not sent thirty-five pounds at the end of last month to pay for mother's treatment in a private hospital, I would have been all right—or if not exactly all right, at least above water. Anyway, I'll pull through," he assured himself. "The beginning was bound to be a little difficult. What do our people say? The start of weeping is always hard. Not a particularly happy proverb, but nonetheless true."

If the Umuofia Progressive Union had granted him four months' grace things might have turned out differently. But all that was now past history. He had made up his quarrel with the Union. It was quite clear they had meant no harm. And even if they had, was it not true, as the President had said at the reconciliation meeting, that anger against a kinsman was felt in the flesh, not in the marrow? The Union had pleaded with him to accept the four months' grace from that moment. But he had refused with the lie that his circumstances were now happier.

And if one thought objectively of the matter—as though it related to Mr. B. and not to one's self—could one blame those poor men for being critical of a senior service man who appeared reluctant to pay twenty pounds a month? They had taxed themselves mercilessly to raise eight hundred pounds to send him to England. Some of them earned no more than five pounds a month. He earned nearly fifty. They had wives and schoolgoing children; he had none. After paying the twenty pounds he would have thirty left. And very soon he would have an increment which alone was as big as some people's salary.

Obi admitted that his people had a sizable point. What they did not know was that, having labored in sweat and tears to enrol their kinsman among the shining élite, they had to keep him there. Having made him a member of an exclusive club whose members greet one another with "How's the car behaving?" did they expect him to turn round and answer: "I'm sorry, but my car is off the road. You see I couldn't pay my insurance premium."? That would be letting the side down in a way that was quite unthinkable. Almost as unthinkable as a masked spirit in the old Ibo society answering another's esoteric salutation: "I'm sorry, my friend, but I don't understand your strange language. I'm but a human being wearing a mask." No, these things could not be.

Ibo people, in their fair-mindedness, have devised a proverb which says that it is not right to ask a man with elephantiasis of the scrotum to take on smallpox as well, when thousands of other people have not had even their share of small diseases. No doubt it is not right. But it happens. "Na so dis world be," they say.

Having negotiated a loan of fifty pounds from the bank and gone straight to hand it over to the insurance company, Obi returned to his office to find his electricity bill for November. When he opened it he came very close to crying. Five pounds seven and three.

"Anything the matter?" asked Miss Tomlinson.

"Oh, no. Not at all." He pulled himself together. "It's only my electricity bill."

"How much do you find it comes to a month?"

"This one is five-seven and three."

"It's sheer robbery what they charge for electricity here. In England you would pay less than that for a whole quarter."

Obi was not in the mood for comparisons. The sudden impact of the insurance notice had woken him up to the real nature of his financial position. He had surveyed the prospects for the next few months and found them pretty alarming. At the end of the month he would have to renew his vehicle license. A whole year was out of the question, but even a quarter alone was four pounds. And then the tires. He could possibly postpone renewing them for another month or so, but they were already as smooth as the tube. Everyone said that it was surprising that his first set of tires did not give him two years or even eighteen months. He could not contemplate four new tires at thirty pounds. So he would have to retread his present set, one at a time beginning with the spare in the boot. That would cut the price down by half. They would probably last only six months as Miss Tomlinson told him. But six months might be long enough for things to improve a little. No one told him about income tax. That was to come, but not for another two months.

As soon as he finished his lunch he immediately set about introducing sweeping economy measures in his flat. His new steward boy, Sebastian, stood by, no doubt wondering what had possessed his master. He had started off his lunch by complaining that there was too much meat in the soup.

"I am not a millionaire, you know," he had said. God knows, Clara used twice as much meat when she made the soup herself! thought Sebastian.

"And in future," Obi continued, "I shall only give you money to go to the market once a week."

Every switch in the flat lit two bulbs. Obi set about pruning them down. The rule in future was to be one switch, one bulb. He had often wondered why there should be two lamps in the bathroom and lavatory. It was typical Government planning. There was no single light on the flight of concrete stairs running through the middle of the block, with the result that people often collided with one another there or slipped one step. And yet there were two lamps in the lavatory where no one wanted to look closely at what one was doing.

Having dealt with the lamps, he turned to Sebastian again. "In future the water heater must not be turned on. I will have cold baths. The fridge must be switched off at seven o'clock in the evening and on again at twelve noon. Do you understand?"

"Yes, sir. But meat no go spoil so?"

"No need to buy plenty meat at once."

"Yes, sir."

"Buy small today; when he finish buy small again."

"Yes, sir. Only I tink you say I go de go market once every week."

"I said nothing of the sort. I said I would only give you money once."

Sebastian now understood. "Na de same ting. Instead to

give me money two times. You go give me now one time."

Obi knew he would not get very far pursuing the matter in the abstract.

That evening he had a serious disagreement with Clara. He had not wanted to tell her about the overdraft, but as soon as she saw him she asked what the matter was. He tried to fob her off with some excuse. But he had not planned it, so it didn't hold together. Clara's way of getting anything from him was not to argue but to refuse to talk. And as she usually did three-quarters of the talking when they were together, the silence soon became too heavy to bear. Obi would then ask her what the matter was, which was usually the prelude to doing whatever she wanted.

"Why didn't you tell me?" she asked when he had told her about the overdraft.

"Well, there was no need. I'll pay it easily in five monthly installments."

"That's not the point. You don't think I should be told when you're in difficulty."

"I wasn't in difficulty. I wouldn't have mentioned it if you hadn't pressed me."

"I see," was all she said. She went across the room and picked up a woman's magazine lying on the floor and began to read.

After a couple of minutes, Obi said with synthetic lightheartedness: "It's very rude to be reading when you have a visitor."

"You should have known I was very badly brought up." Any reflection on her family was a very risky subject and often ended in tears. Even now her eyes were beginning to look glazed.

"Clara," he said, putting his arm round her. She was all tensed up. "Clara." She did not answer. She was turning the pages of the magazine mechanically. "I don't understand why you want to quarrel." Not a sound. "I think I had better be going."

"I think so, too."

"Clara, I'm very sorry."

"About what? Leave me, *ojare*." She pushed his arm off.

Obi sat for another couple of minutes gazing at the floor.

"All right." He sprang to his feet. Clara remained where she was, turning the pages.

"Bye-bye."

"Good-bye."

When he got back to the flat he told Sebastian not to cook any supper.

"I don start already."

"Then you can stop," he shouted, and went into his bedroom. He stopped for a brief moment to look at Clara's photograph on the dressing table. He turned it on its face and went to undress. He threw his cloth over his shoulder, toga-wise, and returned to his sitting room to get a book. He looked along the shelves a number of times without deciding what to read. Then his eye rested on A. E. Housman's *Collected Poems*. He took it down and returned to his bedroom. He picked up Clara's photograph and stood it on its feet again. Then he went and lay down.

He opened the book where a piece of paper was showing, its top frayed and browned from exposure to dust. On it was written a poem called "Nigeria."

> God bless our noble fatherland,
> Great land of sunshine bright,
> Where brave men chose the way of peace,
> To win their freedom fight.
> May we preserve our purity,
> Our zest for life and jollity.

God bless our noble countrymen
And women everywhere.
Teach them to walk in unity
To build our nation dear;
Forgetting region, tribe or speech,
But caring always each for each.

At the bottom was written "London, July 1955." He
smiled, put the piece of paper back where he found it, and
began to read his favorite poem, "Easter Hymn."

CHAPTER ELEVEN

OBI WAS NOW ON THE BEST OF TERMS WITH MISS TOM-
linson. He had begun to lower his guard "small small"
from the day she went into raptures over Clara. She was
now Marie to him and he was Obi to her.

"Miss Tomlinson is rather a mouthful," she had said
one day. "Why not plain Marie?"

"I was going to suggest that myself. But you're not
plain Marie. You are the exact opposite of plain."

"Oh," she said with a delightful jerk of the head.
"Thank you." She stood up and executed a mock curtsy.

They talked, frankly, of many things. Whenever there
was nothing urgent to do, Marie had the habit of folding
her arms and resting them on her typewriter. She would
wait in that posture until Obi raised his eyes from what he
was doing. Mr. Green was usually the subject of discussion, or at least the occasion for starting it. Once started, it
took whatever direction it pleased.

"I had tea with the Greens yesterday," she might say. "They are a most delightful couple, you know. He is quite different at home. Do you know he pays school fees for his steward's sons? But he says the most outrageous things about educated Africans."

"I know," said Obi. "He will make a very interesting case for a psychologist. Charles—you know the messenger—told me that some time ago the A.A. wanted to sack him for sleeping in the office. But when the matter went up to Mr. Green, he tore out the query from Charles's personal file. He said the poor man must be suffering from malaria, and the next day he bought him a tube of quinacrine."

Marie was about to place yet another brick in position in their reconstruction of a strange character when Mr. Green sent for her to take some dictation. She was just saying that he was a very devout Christian, a sidesman at the Colonial Church.

Obi had long come to admit to himself that, no matter how much he disliked Mr. Green, he nevertheless had some admirable qualities. Take, for instance, his devotion to duty. Rain or shine, he was in the office half an hour before the official time, and quite often worked long after two, or returned again in the evening. Obi could not understand it. Here was a man who did not believe in a country, and yet worked so hard for it. Did he simply believe in duty as a logical necessity? He continually put off going to see his dentist because, as he always said, he had some urgent work to do. He was like a man who had some great and supreme task that must be completed before a final catastrophe intervened. It reminded Obi of what he had once read about Mohammed Ali of Egypt, who in his old age worked in frenzy to modernize his country before his death.

In the case of Green it was difficult to see what his deadline was, unless it was Nigeria's independence. They said he had put in his resignation when it was thought that

Nigeria might become independent in 1956. In the event it did not happen and Mr. Green was persuaded to withdraw his resignation.

A most intriguing character, Obi thought, drawing profiles on his blotting pad. One thing he could never draw properly was a shirt collar. Yes, a very interesting character. It was clear he loved Africa, but only Africa of a kind: the Africa of Charles, the messenger, the Africa of his gardenboy and steward boy. He must have come originally with an ideal—to bring light to the heart of darkness, to tribal headhunters performing weird ceremonies and unspeakable rites. But when he arrived, Africa played him false. Where was his beloved bush full of human sacrifice? There was St. George horsed and caparisoned, but where was the dragon? In 1900 Mr. Green might have ranked among the great missionaries; in 1935 he would have made do with slapping headmasters in the presence of their pupils; but in 1957 he could only curse and swear.

With a flash of insight Obi remembered his Conrad which he had read for his degree. "By the simple exercise of our will we can exert a power for good practically unbounded." That was Mr. Kurtz before the heart of darkness got him. Afterwards he had written: "Exterminate all the brutes." It was not a close analogy, of course. Kurtz had succumbed to the darkness, Green to the incipient dawn. But their beginning and their end were alike. "I must write a novel on the tragedy of the Greens of this century," he thought, pleased with his analysis.

Later that morning a ward attendant from the General Hospital brought a little parcel to him. It was from Clara. One of the most wonderful things about her was her writing. It was so feminine. But Obi was not thinking about writing just now. His heart was pounding heavily.

"You may go," he told the ward servant who was waiting to take a message. He started opening the parcel, but stopped again, his hands trembling. Marie was not there at the moment, but she might come in at any time. He thought of taking the parcel to the lavatory. Then a better idea occurred to him. He pulled out one of the drawers and began to untie the parcel inside it. For some reason he knew, despite the size of the parcel, that it contained his ring. And some money too! Yes, five-pound notes. But he didn't see any ring. He sighed with relief and then read the little note enclosed.

Darling,

I'm sorry about yesterday. Go to the bank straight away and cancel that overdraft. See you in the evening.

Love, Clara.

His eyes misted. When he looked up, he saw that Marie was watching him. He hadn't even noticed when she returned to the office.

"What's the matter, Obi?"

"Nothing," he said, improvizing a smile. "I was lost in thought."

Obi wrapped up the fifty pounds carefully and put it in his pocket. How had Clara come by so much money? he wondered. But of course she was reasonably well paid and she had not studied nursing on any progressive union's scholarship. It was true that she sent money to her parents, but that was all. Even so, fifty pounds was a lot of money.

All the way from Ikoyi to Yaba he was thinking how best he could make her take the money back. He knew it was going to be difficult, if not impossible. But it was quite out of the question for him to take fifty pounds from her. The question was how to make her take it back without hurting her. He might say that he would look silly taking an overdraft today and paying it off tomorrow, that the manager might think he had stolen the money. Or he might ask her to keep it until the end of the month, when he would really need it. She might ask: "Why not keep it yourself?" He would answer: "I might spend it before then."

Whenever Obi had a difficult discussion with Clara he planned all the dialogue beforehand. But when the time came it always took a completely different course. And so it did on this occasion. Clara was ironing when he arrived.

"I'll finish in a second," she said. "What did the bank manager say?"

"He was very pleased."

"In future don't be a silly little boy. You know the proverb about digging a new pit to fill up an old one?"

"Why did you trust so much money to that sly-looking man?"

"You mean Joe? He's a great friend of mine. He's a ward servant."

"I didn't like his looks. What is the proverb about digging a new pit to fill up an old one?"

"I have always said you should go and study Ibo. It means borrowing from the bank to pay the insurance."

"I see. You prefer digging two pits to fill up one. Borrowing from Clara to pay the bank to pay the insurance."

Clara made no answer.

"I did not go to the bank. I didn't see how I could. How could I take so much money from you?"

"Please, Obi, stop behaving like a small boy. It is only a loan. If you don't want it you can return it. Actually I have been thinking all afternoon about the whole thing. It seems I have been interfering in your affairs. All I can say is, I'm very sorry. Have you got the money here?" She held out her hand.

Obi took her hand and pulled her towards him. "Don't misunderstand me, darling."

That evening they called on Christopher, Obi's economist friend. Clara had gradually come round to liking him. Perhaps he was a little too lively, which was not a serious fault. But she feared he might influence Obi for the worse in the matter of women. He seemed to enjoy going around with four or five at once. He even said there was nothing like love, at any rate in Nigeria. But he was very likeable really, quite unlike Joseph, who was a bushman.

As was to be expected, Christopher had a girl with him when Clara and Obi arrived. Clara had not met this one before, although apparently Obi had.

"Clara, meet Bisi," said Christopher. The two girls shook hands and said: "Pleased to meet you." "Clara is Obi's——"

"Shut up," Clara completed for him. But it was like trying to complete a sentence for a stammerer. You might as well save your breath.

"Obi's *you know*," completed Christopher.

"Have you been buying new records?" asked Clara, going through a little pile of records on one of the chairs.

"Me? At this time of the month? They are Bisi's. What can I offer you?"

"Champagne."

"Ah? Na Obi go buy you that-o. Me I never reach that grade yet. Na squash me get-o." They laughed.

"Obi, what about some beer?"

"If you'll split a bottle with me."

"Fine. What are you people doing this evening? Make we go dance somewhere?"

Obi tried to make excuses, but Clara cut him short. They would go, she said.

"Na film I wan' go," said Bisi.

"Look here, Bisi, we are not interested in what you want to do. It's for Obi and me to decide. This na Africa, you know."

Whether Christopher spoke good or "broken" English depended on what he was saying, where he was saying it, to whom and how he wanted to say it. Of course that was to some extent true of most educated people, especially on

Saturday nights. But Christopher was rather outstanding in thus coming to terms with a double heritage.

Obi borrowed a tie from him. Not that it mattered at the Imperial, where they had chosen to go. But one didn't want to look like a boma boy.

"Shall we all come into your car, Obi? It's a long time since I had a chauffeur."

"Yes, let's all go together. Although it's going to be difficult after the dance to take Bisi home, then Clara, then you. But it doesn't matter."

"No. I had better bring my car," said Christopher. Then he whispered something into Obi's ear to the effect that he wasn't actually thinking of taking Bisi back that night, which was rather obvious.

"What are you whispering to him?" asked Clara.

"For men only," said Christopher.

There was very little parking space at the Imperial and many cars were already there. After a little to-ing and fro-ing Obi finally squeezed in between two other cars, directed by half a dozen half-clad little urchins who were standing around.

"Na me go look your car for you," chorused three of them at once.

"O.K., make you look am well," said Obi to none in particular. "Lock up your side," he said quietly to Clara.

"I go look am well, sir," said one of the boys, stepping across Obi's path so that he would remark him well as the right person to receive a threepence "dash" at the end of the dance. In principle Obi never gave anything to these juvenile delinquents. But it would be bad policy to tell them so now and then leave your car at their mercy.

Christopher and Bisi were already waiting for them at the gate. The place was not as crowded as they thought it might be. In fact the dance floor was practically empty, but that was because the band was playing a waltz. Christopher found a table and two chairs and the two girls sat.

"You are not going to stand all night," said Clara. "Tell one of the stewards to get you chairs."

"Never mind," said Christopher. "We'll soon get chairs."

He had hardly completed this sentence when the band struck up a high-life. In under thirty seconds the dance floor was invaded. Those who were caught with a glass of beer in midair either put it down again or quickly swallowed its contents. Unfinished cigarettes were, according to the status of the smoker, either thrown on the floor and stepped on or carefully put out, to be continued later.

Christopher moved past three or four tables in front and grabbed two chairs that had just been vacated.

"Mean old thing!" said Obi as he took one. Bisi was wriggling in her chair and singing with the soloist.

> Nylon dress is a lovely dress,
> Nylon dress is a country dress.
> If you want to make your baby happy
> Nylon is good for her.

"We are wasting a good dance," said Obi.

"Why not go and dance with Bisi? Clara and I can watch the chairs."

"Shall we?" Obi said, standing. Bisi was already up with a faraway look in her eyes.

> If you want to make your baby happy
> Go to the shop and get a doz'n of nylon.
> She will know nobody but you alone
> Nylon is good for her.

The next dance was again a high-life. In fact most of the dances were high-lifes. Occasionally a waltz or a blues was played so that the dancers could relax and drink their beer, or smoke. Christopher and Clara danced next while Obi and Bisi kept an eye on their chairs. But soon it was only Obi; someone had asked Bisi to dance.

There were as many ways of dancing the high-life as there were people on the floor. But, broadly speaking, three main patterns could be discerned. There were four or five Europeans whose dancing reminded one of the early motion pictures. They moved like triangles in an alien dance that was ordained for circles. There were others who made very little real movement. They held their women close, breast to breast and groin to groin, so that the dance could flow uninterrupted from one to the other and back again. The last group were the ecstatic ones. They danced apart, spinning, swaying, or doing intricate syncopations with their feet and waist. They were the good servants who had found perfect freedom. The vocalist drew the microphone up to his lips to sing "Gentleman Bobby."

> I was playing moi guitar *jeje*,
> A lady gave me a kiss.
> Her husband didn't like it,
> He had to drag him wife away.
> Gentlemen, please hold your wife.
> Father and mum, please hold your girls.
> The calypso is so nice,
> If they follow, don't blame Bobby.

The applause and the cries of "Anchor! Anchor!" that followed this number seemed to suggest that no one blamed Gentleman Bobby. And why should they? He was playing his guitar *jeje*—quietly, soberly, unobtrusively, altogether in a law-abiding fashion, when a woman took it upon herself to plant a kiss on him. No matter how one looked at it, no blame could possibly attach to the innocent musician.

The next number was a quickstep. In other words, it was time to drink and smoke and generally cool down. Obi ordered soft drinks. He was relieved that no one wanted anything more expensive.

The group on their right—three men and two women—interested him very much. One of the women was quiet, but the other talked all the time at the top of her voice. Her nylon blouse was practically transparent, revealing a new brassière. She had not danced the last number. She had said to the man who asked her: "No petrol, no fire," which clearly meant no beer, no dance. The man had then come to Obi's table and asked Bisi. But that could not be anything like a permanent settlement. Now that no one was dancing, the woman was saying for all to hear: "The table is dry."

At two o'clock Obi and his party rose to go, despite Bisi's reluctance. Christopher reminded her that she had originally elected to go to the films which ended at eleven. She replied that that was no reason why they should leave the dance when it was just beginning to warm up. Anyway, they went. Christopher's car was parked a long way away, so they said good night outside the gate and parted.

Obi opened the driver's door with the key, got in, and leaned sideways to open for Clara. But her door was unlocked.

"I thought you locked this door?"

"Yes, I did," she said.

Panic seized Obi. "Good Lord!" he cried.

"What is it?" She was alarmed.

"Your money."

"Where is it? Where did you leave it?"

He pointed at the now empty glove box. They stared at it in silence. He opened his door quietly, went out, looked vacantly on the ground, and then leaned against the car. The street was completely deserted. Clara opened her door and went out too. She went round to his side of the car, took his hand in hers, and said: "Let's go." He was trembling. "Let's go, Obi," she said again, and opened his door for him.

CHAPTER TWELVE

AFTER CHRISTMAS OBI GOT A LETTER FROM HIS FATHER that his mother was again ill in hospital and to ask when he was coming home on local leave as he had promised. He hoped it would be very soon because there was an urgent matter he must discuss with him.

It was obvious that news had reached them about Clara. Obi had written some months ago to say there was a girl he was interested in and that he would tell them more about her when he got home on two weeks' local leave. He had not told them that she was an *osu*. One didn't write about such things. That would have to be broken very gently in conversation. But now it appeared that someone else had told them.

He folded the letter carefully and put it in his shirt pocket and tried not to think about it, especially about his mother's illness. He tried to concentrate on the file he was reading, but he read every line five times, and even then he did not understand what he read. He took up the telephone to ring Clara at the hospital, but when the operator said "Number, please," he put it down again. Marie was typing steadily. She had plenty of work to do before the next week's board meeting. She was a very good typist; the keys did not strike separately when she typed.

Sometimes Mr. Green sent for Marie to take dictation, sometimes he came out himself to give it. It all depended on how he was feeling at the time. He came out now.

"Please take down a quick answer to this. 'Dear sir, with reference to your letter of—whatever the date was—I beg to inform you that Government pays a dependant's allowance to *bona fide* wives of Government scholars and not to their girl friends. . . .' Will you read that over to me?" Marie did, while he paced up and down. "Change that second *Government* to *its*," he said. Marie made the alteration and then looked up.

"That's all. 'I am your obedient servant, Me.'" Mr. Green always ended his letters that way, saying the words *obedient servant* with a contemptuous tongue in the cheek. He turned to Obi and said: "You know, Okonkwo, I have lived in your country for fifteen years and yet I cannot begin to understand the mentality of the so-called educated Nigerian. Like this young man at the University College, for instance, who expects the Government not only to pay his fees and fantastic allowances and find him an easy, comfortable job at the end of his course, but also to pay his intended. It's absolutely incredible. I think Government is making a terrible mistake in making it so easy for people like that to have so-called university education. Education for what? To get as much as they can for themselves and their family. Not the least bit interested in the millions of their countrymen who die every day from hunger and disease."

Obi made some vague noises.

"I don't expect you to agree with me, of course," said Mr. Green, and disappeared.

Obi rang Christopher and they arranged to go and play tennis that afternoon with two newly arrived teachers at a Roman Catholic convent in Apapa. He had never really found out how Christopher discovered them. All he knew was that about two weeks ago he had been asked to come round to Christopher's flat and meet two Irish girls who were very interested in Nigeria. When Obi had got there at about six Christopher was already teaching them in turns how to dance the high-life. He was obviously relieved when Obi arrived; he immediately appropriated the better-looking of the two girls and left the other to Obi. She was all right when she wasn't trying to smile. Unfortunately she tried to smile rather frequently. But otherwise she wasn't too bad, and very soon it was too dark to see, anyway.

The girls were really interested in Nigeria. They already knew a few words of Yoruba, although they had only been in the country three weeks or so. They were rather more anti-English than Obi, which made him somewhat uneasy. But as the evening wore on he liked them more and more, especially the one assigned to him.

They had fried plantains with vegetable and meat for dinner. The girls said they enjoyed it very much, although it was clear from the running of their eyes and noses that there was too much pepper in it.

They resumed their dancing soon afterwards, in semi-darkness and in silence except when they occasionally teased one another. "Why are you so silent, you two?" or: "Keep moving; don't stand on one spot."

After a few opening skirmishes Obi won a couple of tentative kisses. But when he tried something more ambitious, Nora whispered sharply: "No! Catholics are not allowed to kiss like that."

"Why not?"

"It's a sin."

"How odd."

They continued dancing and occasionally kissing with their lips alone.

Before they finally took them home at eleven Obi and Christopher had promised to go and play tennis with them on some evenings. They had gone twice in quick succession; then other things had claimed their interest. Obi had thought of them again because he wanted something, like a game of tennis, to occupy his mind in the afternoon and perhaps tire him out so that he could sleep at night.

As soon as Christopher's car drew up, a white-clad Mother appeared suddenly at the door of the convent chapel. Obi drew his attention to the fact. She was too far away for them to see the expression on her face, but he felt it was hostile. The girls were having their afternoon prep, and so the convent was very quiet. They went up the stairs that led to Nora and Pat's flat above the classroom, the Mother following them with her eyes until they disappeared into the sitting room.

The girls were having tea and buns. They looked pleased to see their visitors, but somehow not quite as pleased as usual. They seemed a little embarrassed.

"Have some tea," they said together, as if they had been rehearsing the phrase, and before their guests had settled down properly in their chairs. They drank their tea almost in silence. Although Obi and Christopher were dressed for tennis and carried rackets, the girls did not say anything about playing. After tea they sat where they were, attempting valiantly to keep what conversation there was going.

"What about a game?" Christopher asked when the conversation finally expired. There was a pause. Then Nora explained quite simply without any false apologies that the Mother had spoken to them seriously about going around with African men. She had warned them that if the Bishop knew of it they might find themselves sent back to Ireland.

Pat said it was all silly and ridiculous. She actually used the word *ridiculosity*, which made Obi smile internally. "But we don't want to be sent back to Ireland."

Nora promised that they would occasionally go to visit the boys at Ikoyi. But it would be best if they did not come to the convent because the Mother and the Sisters were watching.

"What are you two, anyway? Daughters?" asked Christopher. But this was not very well received and the visit was soon afterwards brought to a close.

"You see," said Christopher as soon as they got back into the car. "And they call themselves missionaries!"

"What do you expect the poor girls to do?"

"I wasn't thinking of them. I mean the Mothers and Sisters and fathers and children."

Obi found himself in the unusual role of defending Roman Catholics.

On their way home they stopped to say hello to Christopher's newest girl friend Florence. He was so taken with her that he even mentioned marriage. But that was impossible because the girl was going to England next September to study nursing. She was out when they got to her place, and Christopher left a note for her.

"I have not seen Bisi for a long time," he said. And they went to see her. But she, too, was out.

"What a day for visits!" said Obi. "We had better go home."

Christopher talked about Florence all the way. Should he try and persuade her not to go to England?

"I shouldn't if I were you," Obi said. He told him of one old catechist in Umuofia many, many years ago when Obi was a little boy. This man's wife was a very good friend of Obi's mother and often visited them. One day he overheard her telling his mother how her education had been cut short at Standard One because the man was impatient to get married. She sounded very bitter about it, although it must have happened at least twenty years before. Obi remembered this particular visit very well because it took place on a Saturday. On the following morning the catechist had been unable to take the service because his wife had broken his head with the wooden pestle used for pounding yams. Obi's father, as a retired catechist, had been asked to conduct the service at very short notice.

"Talking about going to England reminds me of a girl who practically offered herself to me. Have I told you the story?"

"No."

Obi told him the story of Miss Mark, starting with her brother's visit to his office.

"What happened to her in the end?"

"Oh, she is in England. She got the scholarship all right."

"You are the biggest ass in Nigeria," said Christopher, and they began a long argument on the nature of bribery.

"If a girl offers to sleep with you, that is not bribery," said Christopher.

"Don't be silly," replied Obi. "You mean you honestly cannot see anything wrong in taking advantage of a young girl straight from school who wants to go to a university?"

"You are being sentimental. A girl who comes the way she did is not an innocent little girl. It's like the story of the girl who was given a form to fill in. She put down her name and her age. But when she came to sex she wrote: 'Twice a week.' " Obi could not help laughing.

"Don't imagine that girls are angels."

"I was not imagining any such thing. But it is scandalous that a man of your education can see nothing wrong in going to bed with a girl before you let her appear before the board."

"This girl was appearing before the board, anyway. That was all she expected you to do: to see that she did appear. And how do you know she did not go to bed with the board members?"

"She probably did."

"Well, then, what good have you done her?"

"Very little, I admit," said Obi, trying to put his thoughts in order, "but perhaps she will remember that there was one man at least who did not take advantage of his position."

"But she probably thinks you are impotent."

There was a short pause.

"Now tell me, Christopher. What is *your* definition of bribery?"

"Well, let's see. . . . The use of improper influence."

"Good. I suppose——"

"But the point is, there was no influence at all. The girl was going to be interviewed, anyway. She came voluntarily to have a good time. I cannot see that bribery is involved at all."

"Of course, I know you're not really serious."

"I am dead serious."

"But I'm surprised you cannot see that the same argument can be used for taking money. If the applicant is getting the job, anyway, then there is no harm in accepting money from him."

"Well——"

"Well, what?"

"You see, the difference is this." He paused. "Let's put it this way. No man wants to part with his money. If you accept money from a man you make him poorer. But if you go to bed with a girl who asks for it, I don't see that you have done any harm."

They argued over dinner and late into the night. But no sooner had Christopher said good night than Obi's thoughts returned to the letter he had received from his father.

CHAPTER THIRTEEN

OBI WAS GRANTED TWO WEEKS' LOCAL LEAVE FROM 10th to 24th February. He decided to set out for Umuofia very early on the 11th, spend the night at Benin, and conclude the journey the following day. Clara exchanged duties with another nurse so as to be free to help with his packing. She spent the whole day—and the night—in Obi's flat.

When they went to sleep she said she had something to tell him and began to cry. Obi had not learnt to cope with tears; he was always alarmed. "What's the matter, Clara?" But he only got warm tears on the arm which lay between her head and the pillow. Clara cried silently, but Obi could feel from the way her body shook that she was crying violently. He kept asking: "What's the matter? What's the matter?" and getting more and more alarmed.

"Excuse me," she said. She got up and went to the dressing table, where her handbag stood, brought out a handkerchief, and blew her nose. Then she went back to the bed with the handkerchief and sat on the edge.

"Come and tell me what is the trouble," said Obi, gently pulling her down. He kissed her and it tasted salty. "What is it?"

Clara said she was very sorry to let him down at this eleventh hour. But she was sure it would be in everybody's best interest if they broke off their engagement. Obi was deeply stung, but he said nothing for a long time. Afterwards Clara repeated that she was very sorry. There was another long silence.

Then Obi said: "I can understand. . . . It's perfectly all right. . . . I don't blame you in the least." He wanted to add: "Why should you throw yourself away on someone who can't make both ends meet?" But he did not want to sound sentimental. He said instead: "Thank you very much for everything." He sat up in bed. Then he got up altogether and began to pace the room in his pyjamas. It was too dark for Clara to see him—which heightened the effect. But he soon realized that he would have regarded such action, if somebody else had performed it, as cheaply theatrical, and so he stopped and returned to bed, but not close to Clara. He was, however, soon persuaded to move closer and to talk.

Clara begged him not to misunderstand her. She said she was taking her present step because she did not want to ruin his life. "I have thought about the whole matter very carefully. There are two reasons why we should not get married."

"What are they?"

"Well, the first is that your family will be against it. I don't want to come between you and your family."

"Bunk! Anyway, what is the second reason?" She could not remember what it was. It didn't matter, anyway. The first reason was quite enough.

"I'll tell you what the second reason is," said Obi.

"What is it?"

"You don't want to marry someone who has to borrow money to pay for his insurance." He knew it was a grossly unfair and false accusation, but he wanted her to be on the defensive. She nearly started crying again. He pulled her towards him and began to kiss her passionately. She soon responded with equal spirit. "No, no, no! Don't be a naughty boy. . . . You should apologize first for what you said."

"I'm very sorry, darling."

"O.K. I forgive you. No! Wait a minute."

Obi set out just before six in the morning. If Clara had not been there he would not have been able to wake up as early as five-thirty. He felt a little light in the head and heavy in the eyes. He had a cold bath, washing his arms and legs first, then the head, the stomach, and the back in that order. He hated cold baths, but he could not afford to switch on the electric heater, and there was no doubt, he thought as he dried himself, that one felt very brisk after a cold bath. As with weeping, it was only the beginning that was difficult.

Although he had two weeks, he proposed to spend only one at home for reasons of money. To home people, leave meant the return of the village boy who had made good in the town, and everyone expected to share in his good fortune. "After all," they argued, "it was our prayers and our libations that did it for him." They called leave *lifu*, meaning *to squander*.

Obi had exactly thirty-four pounds, nine and three-pence when he set out. Twenty-five pounds was his local leave allowance, which was paid to all senior civil servants for no other reason than that they went on local leave. The rest was the remains of his January salary. With thirty-four pounds one might possibly last two weeks at home, although a man like Obi, with a car and a "European post," would normally be expected to do better. But sixteen pounds ten shillings was to go into brother John's school fees for the second term, which began in April. Obi knew that unless he paid the fees now that he had a lump sum in his pocket he might not be able to do so when the time came.

Obi seemed to look over the shoulders of everyone who came out to welcome him home.

"Where is Mother?" his eyes kept asking. He did not know whether she was still in hospital or at home, and he was afraid to ask.

"Your mother returned from hospital last week," said his father as they entered the house.

"Where is she?"

"In her room," said Eunice, his youngest sister.

Mother's room was the most distinctive in the whole house, except perhaps for Father's. The difficulty in deciding arose from the fact that one could not compare incomparable things. Mr. Okonkwo believed utterly and completely in the things of the white man. And the symbol of the white man's power was the written word, or better still, the printed word. Once before he went to England, Obi heard his father talk with deep feeling about the mystery of the written word to an illiterate kinsman:

"Our women made black patterns on their bodies with

the juice of the *uli* tree. It was beautiful, but it soon faded. If it lasted two market weeks it lasted a long time. But sometimes our elders spoke about *uli* that never faded, although no one had ever seen it. We see it today in the writing of the white man. If you go to the native court and look at the books which clerks wrote twenty years ago or more, they are still as they wrote them. They do not say one thing today and another tomorrow, or one thing this year and another next year. Okoye in the book today cannot become Okonkwo tomorrow. In the Bible Pilate said: 'What is written is written.' It is *uli* that never fades."

The kinsman had nodded his head in approval and snapped his fingers.

The result of Okonkwo's mystic regard for the written word was that his room was full of old books and papers—from Blackie's *Arithmetic,* which he used in 1908, to Obi's Durrell, from obsolete cockroach-eaten translations of the Bible into the Onitsha dialect to yellowed Scripture Union Cards of 1920 and earlier. Okonkwo never destroyed a piece of paper. He had two boxes full of them. The rest were preserved on top of his enormous cupboard, on tables, on boxes and on one corner of the floor.

Mother's room, on the other hand, was full of mundane things. She had her box of clothes on a stool. On the other side of the room were pots of solid palm-oil with which she made black soap. The palm-oil was separated from the clothes by the whole length of the room, because, as she always said, clothes and oil were not kinsmen, and just as it was the duty of clothes to try and avoid oil it was also the duty of the oil to do everything to avoid clothes.

Apart from these two, Mother's room also had such things as last year's coco yams, kola nuts preserved with banana leaves in empty oil pots, palm-ash preserved in an old cylindrical vessel which, as the older children told Obi, had once contained biscuits. In the second stage of its life it had served as a water vessel until it sprang about five leaks which had to be carefully covered with paper before it got its present job.

As he looked at his mother on her bed, tears stood in Obi's eyes. She held out her hand to him and he took it—all bone and skin like a bat's wing.

"You did not see me when I was ill," she said. "Now I am as healthy as a young girl." She laughed without mirth. "You should have seen me three weeks ago. How is your work? Are Umuofia people in Lagos all well? How is Joseph? His mother came to see me yesterday and I told her we were expecting you. . . ."

Obi answered: "They are well, yes, yes and yes." But his heart all the while was bursting with grief.

Later that evening a band of young women who had been making music at a funeral was passing by Okonkwo's house when they heard of Obi's return, and decided to go in and salute him.

Obi's father was up in arms. He wanted to drive them away, but Obi persuaded him that they could do no harm. It was ominous the way he gave in without a fight and went and shut himself up in his room. Obi's mother came out to the *pieze* and sat on a high chair by the window. She liked music even when it was heathen music. Obi stood in the main door, smiling at the singers who had formed themselves on the clean-swept ground outside. As if from a signal the colorful and noisy weaver birds on the tall palm tree flew away in a body, deserting temporarily their scores of brown nests, which looked like giant bootecs.

Obi knew some of the singers well. But there were others who had been married into the village after he had gone to England. The leader of the song was one of them. She had a strong piercing voice that cut the air with a sharp edge. She sang a long recitative before the others joined in. They called it "The Song of the Heart."

A letter came to me the other day.

I said to Mosisi: "Read my letter for me."
Mosisi said to me: "I do not know how to read."
I went to Innocenti and asked him to read my letters.
Innocenti said to me: "I do not know how to read."
I asked Simonu to read for me. Simonu said:
"This is what the letter has asked me to tell you:
He that has a brother must hold him to his heart,
For a kinsman cannot be bought in the market,
Neither is a brother bought with money."

Is everyone here?
(*Hele ee he ee he*)
Are you all here?
(*Hele ee he ee he*)
The letter said
That money cannot buy a kinsman,
(*Hele ee he ee he*)
That he who has brothers
Has more than riches can buy.
(*Hele ee he ee he*)

CHAPTER FOURTEEN

OBI'S SERIOUS TALKS WITH HIS FATHER BEGAN AFTER THE
family had prayed and all but the two of them had gone
to bed. The prayers had taken place in Mother's room
because she was again feeling very weak, and whenever
she was unable to join the others in the parlor her husband conducted prayers in her room.

The devil and his works featured prominently in that
night's prayers. Obi had a shrewd suspicion that his affair
with Clara was one of the works. But it was only a

suspicion; there was nothing yet to show that his parents had actually heard of it.

Mr. Okonkwo's easy capitulation in the afternoon on the matter of heathen singing was quite clearly a tactical move. He let the enemy gain ground in a minor skirmish while he prepared his forces for a great offensive.

He said to Obi after prayers: "I know you must be tired after the great distance you have traveled. There is something important we must talk about, but it can wait until tomorrow, till you have had time to rest."

"We can talk now," said Obi. "I am not too tired. We get used to driving long distances."

"Come to my room, then," said his father, leading the way with the ancient hurricane lamp. There was a small table in the middle of the room. Obi remembered when it was bought. Carpenter Moses had built it and offered it to the church at harvest. It was put up for auction after the Harvest Service and sold. He could not now remember how much his father had paid for it, eleven and three-pence perhaps.

"I don't think there is kerosene in this lamp," said his father, shaking the lamp near his ear. It sounded quite empty. He brought half a bottle of kerosene from his cupboard and poured a little into the lamp. His hands were no longer very steady and he spilt some of the kerosene. Obi did not offer to do it for him because he knew his father would never dream of letting children pour kerosene into his lamp; they would not know how to do it properly.

"How were all our people in Lagos when you left them?" he asked. He sat on his wooden bed while Obi sat on a low stool facing him, drawing lines with his finger on the dusty top of the Harvest table.

"Lagos is a very big place. You can travel the distance from here to Abame and still be in Lagos."

"So they said. But you have a meeting of Umuofia people?" It was half-question, half-statement.

"Yes. We have a meeting. But it is only once a month." And he added: "It is not always that one finds time to attend." The fact was he had not attended since November.

"True," said his father. "But in a strange land one should always move near one's kinsmen." Obi was silent, signing his name in the dust on the table. "You wrote to me some time ago about a girl you had seen. How does the matter stand now?"

"That is one reason why I came. I want us to go and meet her people and start negotiations. I have no money now, but at least we can begin to talk." Obi had decided that it would be fatal to sound apologetic or hesitant.

"Yes," said his father. "That is the best way." He thought a little and again said yes, it was the best way. Then a new thought seemed to occur to him. "Do we know who this girl is and where she comes from?" Obi hesitated just enough for his father to ask the question again in a different way. "What is her name?"

"She is the daughter of Okeke, a native of Mbaino."

"Which Okeke? I know about three. One is a retired teacher, but it would not be that one."

"That is the one," said Obi.

"Josiah Okeke?"

Obi said, yes, that was his name.

His father laughed. It was the kind of laughter one sometimes heard from a masked ancestral spirit. He would salute you by name and ask you if you knew who he was. You would reply with one hand humbly touching the ground that you did not, that he was beyond human knowledge. Then he might laugh as if through a throat of metal. And the meaning of that laughter was clear: "I did not really think you would know, you miserable human worm!"

Obi's father's laughter vanished as it had come—without warning, leaving no footprints.

"You cannot marry the girl," he said quite simply.

"Eh?"

"I said you cannot marry the girl."

"But why, Father?"

"Why? I shall tell you why. But first tell me this. Did you find out or try to find out anything about this girl?"

"Yes."

"What did you find out?"

"That they are *osu*."

"You mean to tell me that you knew, and you ask me why?"

"I don't think it matters. We are Christians." This had some effect, nothing startling though. Only a little pause and a slightly softer tone.

"We are Christians," he said. "But that is no reason to marry an *osu*."

"The Bible says that in Christ there are no bond or free."

"My son," said Okonkwo, "I understand what you say. But this thing is deeper than you think."

"What is *this thing*? Our fathers in their darkness and ignorance called an innocent man *osu*, a thing given to idols, and thereafter he became an outcast, and his children, and his children's children forever. But have we not seen the light of the Gospel?" Obi used the very words that his father might have used in talking to his heathen kinsmen.

There was a long silence. The lamp was now burning too brightly. Obi's father turned down the wick a little and then resumed his silence. After what seemed ages he said: "I know Josiah Okeke very well." He was looking steadily in front of him. His voice sounded tired. "I know him and I know his wife. He is a good man and a great Christian. But he is *osu*. Naaman, captain of the host of Syria, was a great man and honorable, he was also a mighty man of valor, but he was a leper." He paused so that this great and felicitous analogy might sink in with all its heavy and dreadful weight.

"*Osu* is like leprosy in the minds of our people. I beg of you, my son, not to bring the mark of shame and of leprosy into your family. If you do, your children and your children's children unto the third and fourth generations will curse your memory. It is not for myself I speak; my days are few. You will bring sorrow on your head and on the heads of your children. Who will marry your daughters? Whose daughters will your sons marry? Think of that, my son. We are Christians, but we cannot marry our own daughters."

"But all that is going to change. In ten years things will be quite different to what they are now."

The old man shook his head sadly but said no more. Obi repeated his points again. What made an *osu* different from other men and women? Nothing but the ignorance of their forefathers. Why should they, who had seen the light of the Gospel, remain in that ignorance?

He slept very little that night. His father had not appeared as difficult as he had expected. He had not been won over yet, but he had clearly weakened. Obi felt strangely happy and excited. He had not been through anything quite like this before. He was used to speaking to his mother like an equal, even from his childhood, but his father had always been different. He was not exactly remote from his family, but there was something about him that made one think of the patriarchs, those giants hewn from granite. Obi's strange happiness sprang not only from the little ground he had won in the argument, but from the direct human contact he had made with his father for the first time in his twenty-six years.

As soon as he woke up in the morning he went to see his mother. It was six o'clock by his watch, but still very dark. He groped his way to her room. She was awake, for she asked who it was as soon as he entered the room. He went and sat on her bed and felt her temperature with his palm. She had not slept much on account of the pain in her stomach. She said she had now lost faith in the European medicine and would like to try a native doctor.

At that moment Obi's father rang his little bell to summon the family to morning prayers. He was surprised when he came in with the lamp and saw Obi already there. Eunice came in wrapped up in her loincloth. She was the last of the children and the only one at home. That was what the world had come to. Children left their old parents at home and scattered in all directions in search of money. It was hard on an old woman with eight children. It was like having a river and yet washing one's hands with spittle.

Behind Eunice came Joy and Mercy, distant relations who had been sent by their parents to be trained in housekeeping by Mrs. Okonkwo.

Afterwards, when they were alone again, she listened silently and patiently to the end. Then she raised herself up and said: "I dreamt a bad dream, a very bad dream one night. I was lying on a bed spread with white cloth and I felt something creepy against my skin. I looked down on the bed and found that a swarm of white termites had eaten it up, and the mat and the white cloth. Yes, termites had eaten up the bed right under me."

A strange feeling like cold dew descended on Obi's head.

"I did not tell anybody about that dream in the morning. I carried it in my heart wondering what it was. I took down my Bible and read the portion for the day. It gave me some strength, but my heart was still not at rest. In the afternoon your father came in with a letter from Joseph to tell us that you were going to marry an *osu*. I saw the meaning of my death in the dream. Then I told your father about it." She stopped and took a deep breath. "I have nothing to tell you in this matter except one thing. If you want to marry this girl, you must wait until I am no more. If God hears my prayers, you will not wait long." She stopped again. Obi was terrified by the change that had come over her. She looked strange as if she had suddenly gone off her head.

"Mother!" he called, as if she was going away. She held up her hand for silence.

"But if you do the thing while I am alive, you will have my blood on your head, because I shall kill myself." She sank down completely exhausted.

Obi kept to his room throughout that day. Occasionally he fell asleep for a few minutes. Then he would be woken up by the voices of neighbors and acquaintances who came to see him. But he refused to see anybody. He told Eunice to say that he was unwell from long traveling. He knew that it was a particularly bad excuse. If he was unwell, then surely that was all the more reason why he should be seen. Anyway, he refused to be seen, and the neighbors and acquaintances felt wounded. Some of them spoke their mind there and then, others managed to sound as if nothing had happened. One old woman even prescribed a cure for the illness, even though she had not seen the patient. Long journeys, she said, were very troublesome. The thing to do was to take strong purgative medicine to wash out all the odds and ends in the belly.

Obi did not appear for evening prayers. He heard his father's voice as if from a great distance, going on for a very long time. Whenever it appeared to have finished, his voice rose again. At last Obi heard several voices saying the Lord's Prayer. But everything sounded far away, as voices and the cries of insects sound to a man in a fever.

His father came into his room with his hurricane lamp and asked how he felt. Then he sat down on the only chair in the room, took up his lamp again and shook it for kerosene. It sounded satisfactory and he turned the wick down, until the flame was practically swallowed up in the lamp's belly. Obi lay perfectly still on his back, looking up at the bamboo ceiling, the way he had been told as a child not to sleep. For it was said if he slept on his back and a spider crossed the ceiling above him he would have bad dreams.

He was amazed at the irrelevant thoughts that passed through his mind at this the greatest crisis in his life. He waited for his father to speak that he might put up another fight to justify himself. His mind was troubled not only by what had happened but also by the discovery that there was nothing in him with which to challenge it honestly. All day he had striven to rouse his anger and his conviction, but he was honest enough with himself to realize that the response he got, no matter how violent it sometimes appeared, was not genuine. It came from the periphery and not the center, like the jerk in the leg of a dead frog when a current is applied to it. But he could not accept the present state of his mind as final, so he searched desperately for something that would trigger off the inevitable reaction. Perhaps another argument with his father, more violent than the first; for it was true what the Ibos say, that when a coward sees a man he can beat he becomes hungry for a fight. He had discovered he could beat his father.

But Obi's father sat in silence, declining to fight. Obi turned on his side and drew a deep breath. But still his father said nothing.

"I shall return to Lagos the day after tomorrow," Obi said finally.

"Did you not say you had a week to spend with us?"

"Yes, but I think it will be better if I return earlier."

After this there was another long silence. Then his father spoke, but not about the thing that was on their minds. He began slowly and quietly, so quietly that his words were barely audible. It seemed as if he was not really speaking to Obi. His face was turned sideways so that Obi saw it in vague profile.

"I was no more than a boy when I left my father's house and went with the missionaries. He placed a curse on me. I was not there but my brothers told me it was true. When a man curses his own child it is a terrible thing. And I was his first son."

Obi had never heard about the curse. In broad daylight and in happier circumstances he would not have attached any importance to it. But that night he felt strangely moved with pity for his father.

"When they brought me word that he had hanged himself I told them that those who live by the sword must perish by the sword. Mr. Braddeley, the white man who was our teacher, said it was not the right thing to say and told me to go home for the burial. I refused to go. Mr. Braddeley thought I spoke about the white man's messenger whom my father killed. He did not know I spoke about Ikemefuna, with whom I grew up in my mother's hut until the day came when my father killed him with his own hands." He paused to collect his thoughts, turned in his chair, and faced the bed on which Obi lay. "I tell you all this so that you may know what it was in those days to become a Christian. I left my father's house, and he placed a curse on me. I went through fire to become a Christian. Because I suffered I understand Christianity—more than you will ever do." He stopped rather abruptly. Obi thought it was a pause, but he had finished.

Obi knew the sad story of Ikemefuna who was given to Umuofia by her neighbors in appeasement. Obi's father and Ikemefuna became inseparable. But one day the Oracle of the Hills and the Caves decreed that the boy should be killed. Obi's grandfather loved the boy. But when the moment came it was his matchet that cut him down. Even in those days some elders said it was a great wrong that a man should raise his hands against a child that called him father.

CHAPTER FIFTEEN

OBI DID THE 500-ODD MILES BETWEEN UMUOFIA AND Lagos in a kind of daze. He had not even stopped for lunch at Akure, which was the normal halfway house for travelers from Eastern Nigeria to Lagos, but had driven numbly, mile after mile, from morning till evening. Only once did the journey come alive, just before Ibadan. He had taken a sharp corner at speed and come face to face with two mammy-wagons, one attempting to overtake the other. Less than half a second lay between Obi and a total smash. In that half-second he swerved his car into the bush on the left.

One of the lorries stopped, but the other went on its way. The driver and passengers of the good lorry rushed to see what had happened to him. He himself did not know yet whether anything had happened to him. They helped him push his car out, much to the joy of the women passengers who were already crying and holding their breasts. It was only after Obi had been pushed back to the road that he began to tremble.

"You very lucky-o," said the driver and his passengers, some in English and others in Yoruba. "Dese reckless drivers," he said shaking his head sadly. "*Olorun!*" He left the matter in the hands of God. "But you lucky-o as no big tree de for dis side of road. When you reach home make you tank your God."

Obi examined his car and found no damage except one or two little dents.

132

"Na Lagos you de go?" asked the driver. Obi nodded, still unable to talk.

"Make you take am *jeje*. Too much devil de for dis road. If you see one accident way we see for Abeokuta side—*Olorun!*" The women talked excitedly, with their arms folded across their breasts, gazing at Obi as if he was a miracle. One of them repeated in broken English that Obi must thank God. A man agreed with her. "Na only by God of power na him make you still de talk." Actually Obi wasn't talking, but the point was cogent nonetheless.

"Dese drivers! Na waya for dem."

"No be all drivers de reckless," said the good driver. "Dat one na foolish somebody. I give am signal make him no overtake but he just come *fiam*." The last word, combined with a certain movement of the arm meant *excessive speed*.

The rest of the journey had passed without incident. It was getting dark when Obi arrived in Lagos. The big signboard which welcomes motorists to the federal territory of Lagos woke in him a feeling of panic. During the last night he spent at home he had worked out how he was going to tell Clara. He would not go to his flat first and then return to tell her. It would be better to stop on his way and take her with him. But when he got to Yaba where she lived he decided that it was better to get home first and then return. So he passed.

He had a wash and changed his clothes. Then he sat down on the sofa and for the first time felt really tired. Another thought occurred to him. Christopher might be able to give him useful advice. He got into the car and drove off, not knowing definitely whether he was going to Christopher's or Clara's. But in the end it was to Clara that he went.

On his way he ran into a long procession of men, women, and children in white flowing gowns gathered at the waist with red and yellow sashes. The women, who were in the majority, wore white head ties that descended to their back. They sang and clapped their hands and danced. One of the men kept beat with a handbell. They held up all traffic, for which Obi was inwardly grateful. But impatient taxi drivers serenaded them with long and deafening blasts of their horns as they slowly parted for them to pass. In front two white-clad boys carried a banner which proclaimed the Eternal Sacred Order of Cherubim and Seraphim.

Obi had done his best to make the whole thing sound unimportant. Just a temporary setback and no more. Everything would work out nicely in the end. His mother's mind had been affected by her long illness but she would soon get over it. As for his father, he was as good as won over. "All we need do is lie quiet for a little while," he said.

Clara had listened in silence, rubbing her engagement ring with her right fingers. When he stopped talking, she looked up at him and asked if he had finished. He did not answer.

"Have you finished?" she asked again.

"Finished what?"

"Your story."

Obi drew a deep breath by way of answer.

"Don't you think . . . Anyway, it doesn't matter. There is only one thing I regret. I should have known better anyway. It doesn't really matter."

"What are you talking about, Clara? . . . Oh, don't be silly," he said as she pulled off her ring and held it out to him.

"If you don't take it, I shall throw it out of the window."

"Please do."

She didn't throw it away, but went outside to his car and dropped it in the glove box. She came back and, holding out her hand in mock facetiousness, said: "Thank you very much for everything."

"Come and sit down, Clara. Let's not be childish. And please don't make things more difficult for me."

"You are making things difficult for yourself. How many times did I tell you that we were deceiving ourselves? But I was always told I was being childish. Anyway, it doesn't matter. There is no need for long talk."

Obi sat down again. Clara went to lean on the window and look outside. Once Obi began to say something, but gave it up after the first three words or so. After another ten minutes of silence Clara asked, hadn't he better be going?

"Yes," he said, and got up.

"Good night." She did not turn from her position. She had her back to him.

"Good night," he said.

"There was something I wanted to tell you, but it doesn't matter. I ought to have been able to take care of myself."

Obi's heart flew into his mouth. "What is it?" he asked in great alarm.

"Oh, nothing. Forget about it. I'll find a way out."

Obi had been shocked by the crudity of Christopher's reaction to his story. He said the most uncharitable things, and he was always interrupting. As soon as Obi mentioned his parents' opposition he took over from him.

"You know, Obi," he said, "I had wanted to discuss that matter with you. But I have learnt not to interfere in a matter between a man and a woman, especially with chaps like you who have wonderful ideas about love. A friend came to me last year and asked my advice about a girl he wanted to marry. I knew this girl very very well. She is, you know, very liberal. So I told my friend: 'You shouldn't marry this girl.' Do you know what this bloody fool did? He went and told the girl what I said. That was why I didn't tell you anything about Clara. You may say that I am not broad-minded, but I don't think we have reached the stage where we can ignore all our customs. You may talk about education and so on, but I am not going to marry an *osu*."

"We're not talking about your marriage now."

"I'm sorry. What did your mother actually say?"

"She really frightened me. She said I should wait until she is dead, or else she would kill herself."

Christopher laughed. "There was one woman in my place who returned from market one day and found that her two children had fallen into a well and drowned. She wept throughout that day and the next saying that she wanted to go and fall into the well, too. But of course her neighbors held her back every time she got up. But after three days her husband got rather fed up and ordered that she should be left alone to do what she liked. She rushed to the well, but when she got there she first had a peep and then she put her right foot in, brought it out, and put her left . . ."

"How interesting!" Obi said, interrupting him. "But I can assure you my mother meant every word she said. Anyway, what I came to ask you about is quite different. I think she is pregnant."

"Who?"

"Don't be silly. Clara."

"Well, well, that is going to be troublesome."

"Do you know of any . . ."

"Doctor? No. But I know that James went to see one or two of them when he got into trouble recently. I tell you what. I'll find out from him tomorrow morning and give you a ring."

"Not my telephone!"

"Why not? I shall only read out addresses. It's going to cost you some money. Of course you will say I am callous, but my attitude to these things is quite different. When I was in the East a girl came to me and said: 'I can't find my period.' I said to her: 'Go and look for it.' It sounds callous, but . . . I don't know. The way I look at it is this: how do I know that I am responsible? I make sure that I take every possible precaution. That's all. I know that your case is quite different. Clara had no time for any other person. But even so . . ."

There must have been something about Obi which made the old doctor uneasy. He had seemed willing enough at the beginning, and actually asked one or two sympathetic questions. Then he went into an inner room and when he came out he was a changed man.

"I am sorry, my dear young man," he said, "but I cannot help you. What you are asking me to do is a criminal offense for which I could go to jail and lose my license. But apart from that I have my reputation to safeguard—twenty years' practice without a single blot. How old are you?"

"Twenty-six."

"Twenty-six. So you were six years old when I began to practice medicine. And in all those years I have not had anything to do with these shady things. Why don't you marry the girl anyway? She is very good-looking."

"I don't want to marry him," said Clara sullenly, the first thing she had said since they came in.

"What's wrong with him? He seems a nice young man to me."

"I say I won't marry him. Isn't that enough?" she almost screamed, and rushed out of the room. Obi went quietly after her and they drove off. No single word passed between them all the way to the house of the next doctor who had been recommended to Obi.

He was young and very businesslike. He said he had no taste for the kind of job they were asking him to do. "It is not medicine," he said. "I did not spend seven years in England to study *that*. However, I shall do it for you if you are prepared to pay my fee. Thirty pounds. To be paid before I do anything. No checks. Raw cash. What say you?"

Obi asked if he wouldn't take anything less than thirty pounds.

"I'm sorry, but my price is fixed. It is a very minor operation, but it is a crime. We are all criminals, you know. I'm taking a big risk. Go and think about it and come back tomorrow at two, with the money." He rubbed his hands together in a way that struck Obi as particularly sinister. "If you are coming," he said to Clara, "you must not eat."

As they were leaving he asked Obi: "Why don't you marry her?" He received no answer.

CHAPTER SIXTEEN

THE MOST IMMEDIATE PROBLEM WAS HOW TO RAISE THIRTY pounds before two o'clock the next day. There was also Clara's fifty pounds which he must return. But that could wait. The simplest thing would be to go to a moneylender, borrow thirty pounds and sign that he had received sixty. But he would commit suicide before he went to a moneylender.

He had already checked on what was left of the money he took home. He went to his box and checked again. It was twelve pounds in notes plus some loose coins he carried in his pocket. He had given only five pounds for his mother and nothing to his father because he had decided that, as things were, he must find Clara's fifty pounds quite soon.

It would be pointless asking Christopher. His salary never went beyond the tenth of the month. The only thing that saved him from starvation was the brilliant system he had evolved with his cook. At the beginning of every month Christopher gave him all the "chop money" for the month. "Until the next pay day," he would say, "my life is in your hands."

Obi once asked him what would happen if the man absconded with the money halfway through the month. Christopher said he knew he wouldn't. It was most unusual for a "master" to have so much confidence in his "boy," even when, as in this case, the boy was almost twice the master's age and treated him as a son.

In his extremity Obi even thought of the President of the Umuofia Progressive Union. But rather than do that he would go to a moneylender. Apart from the fact that the President would want to know why a young man in the senior service should want to borrow money from a man of family on less than half his salary, it would appear as if Obi had accepted the principle that his townpeople could tell him whom not to marry. "I haven't descended so low yet," he said aloud.

At last a very good idea struck him. Perhaps it wasn't all that good when you came to look at it closely, but it was much better than all the other ideas. He would ask the Hon. Sam Okoli. He would tell him quite frankly what he needed the money for and that he would repay in three months' time. Or perhaps he should not tell him what he needed the money for. It was not fair on Clara to tell even one person more than was absolutely necessary. He had only told Christopher because he thought he might know what doctors to consult. As soon as he had got back to his flat that evening it had occurred to him that he had not stressed the need for secrecy and he had rushed to the telephone. There was only one telephone for the block of six flats but it was just outside his door.

"Hello. Oh, yes, Chris. I forgot to mention it. When you are getting the addresses from that chap don't tell him who it's for. . . . Not for my sake, but . . . you know."

Christopher told him, fortunately in Ibo, that pregnancy could not be covered with the hand.

Obi told him not to be a bloody fool. "Yes, tomorrow morning. Not at the office, no, here. I'm not starting work till next week, Wednesday. Oh, yes. Many thanks. Byebye."

The doctor counted his wad of notes carefully, folded it, and put it in his pocket. "Come back at five o'clock," he told Obi, dismissing him. But when Obi got to his car he could not drive away. All kinds of frightening thoughts kept crowding into his mind. He did not believe in premonition and such stuff, but somehow he felt that he wasn't going to see Clara again.

As he sat in the driver's seat, paralyzed by his thoughts, the doctor and Clara came out and entered a car that was parked by the side of the road. The doctor must have said something about him because Clara looked in his direction once and immediately took her eyes away. Obi wanted to rush out of his car and shout: "Stop. Let's go and get married now," but he couldn't and didn't. The doctor's car drove away.

It could not have been more than a minute, or at most two. Obi's mind was made up. He reversed his car and chased after the doctor's to stop them. But they were no longer in sight. He tried first one turning and then another. He dashed across a major road and was missed by a huge red bus by a hair's breadth. He backed, went forward, turned right and left like a panicky fly trapped behind the windscreen. Cyclists and pedestrians cursed him. At one stage the whole of Lagos rose in one loud protest: "ONE WAY! ONE WAY!!" He stopped, backed into a side street, and then went in the opposite direction.

After about half an hour of this mad and aimless exercise Obi pulled up by the side of the road. He felt in his right pocket, then in his left for a handkerchief. Finding none, he rubbed his eyes with the back of his hand.

Then he placed his arms on the steering wheel and put his head on them. His face and arms gradually became wet where they came in contact, and dripped with sweat. It was the worst time of the day and the worst time of the year—the last couple of months before the rains broke. The air was dead, heavy and hot. It lay on the earth like a mantle of lead. Inside Obi's car it was worse. He had not wound down the glass at the back and the heat was trapped inside. He did not notice it, but even if he had noticed it he would not have done anything about it.

At five o'clock he returned to the clinic. The doctor's attendant said he was out. Obi asked if she knew where he had gone. The girl answered a curt "no."

"There is something very important that I must tell him. Can't you try and find him for me . . . or . . ."

"I don't know where he has gone to," she said. Her accent was about as gentle as the splitting of hard wood with an axe.

Obi waited for an hour and a half before the doctor returned—without Clara. Sweat rained down his body.

"Oh, are you here?" the doctor asked. "Come back tomorrow morning."

"Where is she?"

"Don't worry, she will be all right. But I want to have her under observation tonight in case of complications."

"Can't I see her?"

"No. Tomorrow morning. That is, if she wants to see you. Women are very funny creatures, you know."

He told his houseboy Sebastian not to cook supper.

"Master no well?"

"No."

"Sorry, sir."

"Thank you. Go away now. I'll be all right in the morning."

He wanted a book to look at, so he went to his shelf. The pessimism of A. E. Housman once again proved

irresistible. He took it down and went to his bedroom.
The book opened at the place where he had put the paper
on which he had written the poem "Nigeria" in London
about two years ago.

> God bless our noble fatherland
> Great land of sunshine bright,
> Where brave men chose the way of peace,
> To win their freedom fight.
> May we preserve our purity,
> Our zest for life and jollity.

> God bless our noble countrymen
> And women everywhere.
> Teach them to work in unity
> To build our nation dear;
> Forgetting region, tribe or speech,
> But caring always each for each.
>> London, July 1955.

He quietly and calmly crumpled the paper in his left
palm until it was a tiny ball, threw it on the floor, and
began to turn the pages of the book forwards and back-
wards. In the end he did not read any poem. He put the
book down on the little table by his bed.

The doctor was seeing new patients in the morning. They
sat on two long forms in the corridor and went in one by
one behind the green door blinds of the consulting room.
Obi told the attendant that he was not a patient and that
he had an urgent appointment with the doctor. It was not
the same attendant as he had met on the previous day.

"What kin' appointment you get with doctor when you
no be patient?" she asked. Some of the waiting patients
laughed and applauded her wit.

"Man way no sick de come see doctor?" she repeated
for the benefit of those on whom the subtlety of the
original statement might have been lost.

Obi paced up and down the corridor until the doctor's bell rang again. The attendant tried to block his way. He pushed her aside and went in. She rushed in after him to protest that he had jumped the queue. But the doctor paid no attention to her.

"Oh, yes," he said to Obi after a second or two's hesitation as if trying to remember where he had seen that face before. "She is at a private hospital. You remember I told you some of them develop complications. But there is nothing to worry about. A friend of mine is looking after her in his hospital." He gave him the name of the hospital.

When Obi came out, one of the patients was waiting to have a word with him.

"You tink because Government give you car you fit do what you like? You see all of we de wait here and you just go in. You tink na play we come play?"

Obi passed on without saying a word.

"Foolish man. He tink say because him get car so derefore he can do as he like. Beast of no nation!"

In the hospital a nurse told Obi that Clara was very ill and that visitors were not allowed to see her.

CHAPTER SEVENTEEN

"DID YOU HAVE A GOOD LEAVE?" MR. GREEN ASKED WHEN he saw Obi. It was so unexpected that for a little while Obi was too confused to answer. But he managed in the end to say that he did, thank you very much.

"It often amazes me how you people can have the

effrontery to ask for local leave. The idea of local leave was to give Europeans a break to go to a cool place like Jos or Buea. But today it is completely obsolete. But for an African like you, who has too many privileges as it is, to ask for two weeks to go on a swan, it makes me want to cry."

Obi said he wouldn't be worried if local leave was abolished. But that was for Government to decide.

"It's people like you who ought to make the Government decide. That is what I have always said. There is no single Nigerian who is prepared to forgo a little privilege in the interests of his country. From your ministers down to your most junior clerk. And you tell me you want to govern yourselves."

The talk was cut short by a telephone call for Mr. Green. He returned to his room to take it.

"There's a lot of truth in what he says," Marie ventured after a suitable interval.

"I'm sure there is."

"I don't mean about you, or anything of the sort. But quite frankly, there are too many holidays here. Mark you, I don't really mind. But in England I never got more than two weeks' leave in the year. But here, what is it? Four months." At this point Mr. Green returned.

"It is not the fault of Nigerians," said Obi. "You devised these soft conditions for yourselves when every European was automatically in the senior service and every African automatically in the junior service. Now that a few of us have been admitted into the senior service, you turn round and blame us." Mr. Green passed on to Mr. Omo's office next door.

"I suppose so," said Marie, "but surely it's time someone stopped all the Moslem holidays."

"Nigeria is a Moslem country, you know."

"No, it isn't. You mean the North."

They argued for a little while longer and Marie suddenly changed the subject.

"You look run down, Obi."

"I have not been very well."

"Oh, I'm sorry. What is it? Fever?"

"Yes, a slight touch of malaria."

"Why don't you take paludrine?"

"I sometimes forget."

"Tut-tut," she said. "You ought to be ashamed of yourself. And what does your fiancée say? She is a nurse, isn't she?"

Obi nodded.

"If I were you, I should go and see a doctor. You do look ill, believe me."

Later that morning Obi went to consult Mr. Omo about a salary advance. Mr. Omo was the authority on General Orders and Financial Instructions, and should be able to tell him whether such a thing was possible and under what conditions. He had taken a firm decision about Clara's fifty pounds. He must find it in the next two months and pay it into her bank. Perhaps they would get over the present crisis, perhaps not. But whatever happened, he must return the money.

He had at last succeeded in seeing her at the hospital. But as soon as she saw him she had turned on her bed and faced the wall. There were other patients in the ward and most of them saw what had happened. Obi had never felt so embarrassed in his life. He left at once.

Mr. Omo said it was possible to give an officer a salary advance under special conditions. The way he said it, it appeared the special conditions were not unconnected with his personal pleasure.

"And by the way," he said dropping the matter of advance, "you have to submit statement of expenditure in respect of the twenty-five pounds and refund the balance."

Obi had not realized that the allowance was not a free gift to be spent as one liked. He now learnt to his horror that, subject to a maximum of twenty-five pounds, he was allowed to claim so much for every mile of the return journey. Mr. Omo called it claiming "on an actuality basis."

Obi returned to his desk to do a little arithmetic, using the mileage chart. He discovered that the return journey from Lagos to Umuofia amounted to only fifteen pounds. "That's just too bad," he thought. Mr. Omo should have warned him when he gave him twenty-five. Anyway, it was too late to do anything about it now. He couldn't possibly refund ten pounds. He would have to say that he spent his leave in the Cameroons. Pity, that.

The chief result of the crisis in Obi's life was that it made him examine critically for the first time the mainspring of his actions. And in doing so he uncovered a good deal that he could only regard as sheer humbug. Take this matter of twenty pounds every month to his town union, which in the final analysis was the root cause of all his troubles. Why had he not swallowed his pride and accepted the four months' exemption which he had been allowed, albeit with a bad grace? Could a person in his position afford that kind of pride? Was it not a common saying among his people that a man should not, out of pride and etiquette, swallow his phlegm?

Having seen the situation in its true light, Obi decided to stop payment forthwith until such a time as he could do it conveniently. The question was: Should he go and tell his town union? He decided against that, too. He would not give them another opportunity to pry into his affairs. He would just stop paying and, if they asked him why, he would say he had some family commitments which he must clear first. Everyone understood family commitments and would sympathize. If they didn't it was just too bad. They would not take a kinsman to court, not for that kind of reason anyway.

As he turned these things over in his mind the door opened and a messenger entered. Involuntarily Obi jumped to his feet to accept an envelope. He looked it over and turned it round and saw that it had not been opened. He put it in his shirt pocket and sank to his seat. The messenger had vanished as soon as he delivered the letter.

His decision to write to Clara had been taken last night. Thinking again about the hospital incident, Obi had come to the conclusion that his anger was not justified. Or at any rate, Clara had far more to be angry about than he had. She was no doubt thinking that it was no thanks to him that she was still alive. She could not, of course, know how many anxious days and sleepless nights that he had passed through. But even if she did, would she be impressed? What comfort did a dead man derive from the knowledge that his murderer was in sackcloth and ashes?

Obi, who nowadays spent all his time in bed, had got himself out and gone to his writing desk. Writing letters did not come easily to him. He worked out every sentence in his mind first before he set it down on paper. Sometimes he spent as long as ten minutes on the opening sentence. He wanted to say: "Forgive me for what has happened. It was all my fault. . . ." He ruled against it; that kind of self-reproach was sheer humbug. In the end he wrote:

"I can understand your not wanting ever to set eyes on me again. I have wronged you terribly. But I cannot believe that it is all over. If you give me another chance, I shall never fail you again."

He read it over and over again. Then he rewrote the whole letter, changing *I cannot believe* to *I cannot bring myself to believe.*

He left home very early in the morning so that he could drop the letter at the hospital before reporting for duty at eight o'clock. He dared not go into the ward; he stood outside waiting for a nurse to show up. Large numbers of patients were already queueing up in front of the consulting room. The air smelt of carbolic and strange drugs. Perhaps the hospital wasn't really dirty, although it looked so. A little to the right a pregnant woman was vomiting into an open drain. Obi did not want to see the vomit, but his eyes kept wandering there on their own account.

Two ward servants passed by Obi and he heard one say to the other:

"Wetin de sick dat nursing sister?"

"Me I no know-o," the other answered as if he had been charged with complicity. "Dis kind well today sick tomorrow pass me."

"Dey say dey don givam belle."

CHAPTER EIGHTEEN

ALTOGETHER CLARA WAS IN HOSPITAL FOR FIVE WEEKS. As soon as she was discharged she was granted seventy days' leave and she left Lagos. Obi heard of it from Christopher, who heard of it from his girl friend who was a nurse in the General Hospital.

After one more failure Obi had been advised not to try to see Clara again in her present frame of mind. "She will come round," said Christopher. "Give her time." Then he quoted in Ibo the words of encouragement which the bedbug was said to have spoken to her children when hot water was poured on them all. She told them not to lose heart because whatever was hot must in the end turn cold.

Obi's plan to pay fifty pounds into her account had come to nothing for various reasons. One day he had received a registered parcel slip. He wondered who could be sending him a registered parcel. It turned out to have been the Commissioner of Income Tax.

Marie advised him to arrange in future to pay by monthly installments through his bank. "That way you don't notice it," she said.

That was, of course, useful advice for the next tax year. As for the present, he had to find thirty-two pounds pretty soon.

On top of it all came his mother's death. He sent all he could find for her funeral, but it was already being said to his eternal shame that a woman who had borne so many children, one of whom was in a European post, deserved a better funeral than she got. One Umuofia man who had been on leave at home when she died had brought the news to Lagos to the meeting of the Umuofia Progressive Union.

"It was a thing of shame," he said. Someone else wanted to know, by the way, why that beast (meaning Obi) had not obtained permission to go home. "That is what Lagos can do to a young man. He runs after sweet things, dances breast to breast with women and forgets his home and his people. Do you know what medicine that *osu* woman may have put into his soup to turn his eyes and ears away from his people?"

"Do you ever see him in our meetings these days?" asked another. "He has found better company."

At this stage one of the older members of the meeting raised his voice. He was a very pompous man.

"Everything you have said is true. But there is one thing I want you to learn. Whatever happens in this world has a meaning. As our people say: 'Wherever something stands, another thing stands beside it.' You see this thing called blood. There is nothing like it. That is why when you plant a yam it produces another yam, and if you plant an orange it bears oranges. I have seen many things in my life, but I have never yet seen a banana tree yield a coco yam. Why do I say this? You young men here, I want you to listen because it is from listening to old men that you learn wisdom. I know that when I return to

Umuofia I cannot claim to be an old man. But here in this Lagos I am an old man to the rest of you." He paused for effect. "This boy that we are all talking about, what has he done? He was told that his mother died and he did not care. It is a strange and surprising thing, but I can tell you that I have seen it before. His father did it."

There was some excitement at this. "Very true," said another old man.

"I say that his father did the same thing," said the first man very quickly, lest the story be taken from his mouth. "I am not guessing and I am not asking you not to mention it outside. When this boy's father—you all know him, Isaac Okonkwo—when Isaac Okonkwo heard of the death of his father he said that those who kill with the matchet must die by the matchet."

"Very true," said the other man again. "It was the talk of Umuofia in those days and for many years. I was a very little boy at the time, but I heard of it."

"You see that," said the President. "A man may go to England, become a lawyer or a doctor, but it does not change his blood. It is like a bird that flies off the earth and lands on an anthill. It is still on the ground."

Obi had been utterly prostrated by the shock of his mother's death. As soon as he saw a post office messenger in khaki and steel helmet walking towards his table with the telegram he had known.

His hand trembled violently as he signed the receipt and the result was nothing like his signature.

"Time of receipt," said the messenger.

"What is the time?"

"You get watch."

Obi looked at his watch, for, as the messenger had pointed out, he had one.

Everybody was most kind. Mr. Green said he could take a week's leave if he wished. Obi took two days. He went straight home and locked himself up in his flat.

What was the point in going to Umuofia? She would have been buried by the time he got there, anyway. The thought of going home and not finding her! In the privacy of his bedroom he let tears run down his face like a child.

The effect of his tears was startling. When he finally went to sleep he did not wake up even once in the night. Such a thing had not happened to him for many years. In the last few months he had hardly known any sleep at all.

He woke with a start and saw that it was broad daylight. For a brief moment he wondered what had happened. Then yesterday's thought woke violently. Something caught in his throat. He got out of bed and stood gazing at the light coming in through the louvres. Shame and guilt filled his heart. Yesterday his mother had been put into the ground and covered with red earth and he could not keep as much as one night's vigil for her.

"Terrible!" he said. His thoughts went to his father. Poor man, he would be completely lost without her. For the first month or so it would not be too bad. Obi's married sisters would all return home. Esther could be relied upon to look after him. But in the end they would all have to go away again. That was the time the blow would really fall—when everyone began to go away. Obi wondered whether he had done the right thing in not setting out for Umuofia yesterday. But what could have been the point in going? It was more useful to send all the money he could for the funeral instead of wasting it on petrol to get home.

He washed his head and face and shaved with an old razor. Then he nearly burnt his mouth out by brushing his teeth with shaving cream which he mistook for toothpaste.

As soon as he returned from the bank he went and lay down again. He did not get up until Joseph came at about three in the afternoon. He came in a taxi. Sebastian opened the door for him.

"Put these bottles in the fridge," he told him.

Obi came out from his bedroom and found bottles of beer at the doorstep. There must have been a dozen. "What is that, Joseph?" he asked. Joseph did not reply immediately. He was helping Sebastian to put them away first.

"They are mine," he said at last. "I will use them for something."

Before very long a number of Umuofia people began to arrive. Some came in taxis, not singly like Joseph but in teams of three or four, sharing the fare among them. Others came on bicycles. Altogether there were over twenty-five.

The President of the Umuofia Progressive Union asked whether is was permissible to sing hymns in Ikoyi. He asked because Ikoyi was a European reservation. Obi said he would rather they did not sing, but he was touched most deeply that so many of his people had come, in spite of everything, to condole with him. Joseph called him aside and told him in a whisper that he had brought the beer to help him entertain those who would come.

"Thank you," Obi said, fighting back the mist which threatened to cover his eyes.

"Give them about eight bottles, and keep the rest for those who will come tomorrow."

Everybody on arrival went to Obi and said *"Ndo"* to him. He answered some with a word and some with a nod of the head. No one dwelt unduly on his sorrow. They simply told him to take heart and were soon talking about the normal affairs of life. The news of the day was about the Minister of Land who used to be one of the most popular politicians until he took it into his head to challenge the national hero.

"He is a foolish somebody," said one of the men in English.

"He is like the little bird *nza* who after a big meal so far forgot himself as to challenge his *chi* to single combat," said another in Ibo.

"What he saw in Obodo will teach him sense," said yet another. "He went to address his people, but everyone in the crowd covered his nose with a handkerchief because his words stank."

"Was that not where they beat him?" asked Joseph.

"No, that was in Abame. He went there with lorry-loads of women supporters. But you know Abame people; they don't waste time. They beat him up well well and seized his women's head ties. They said it was not proper to beat women, so they took their head ties from them."

In the far corner a little group was having a different conversation. There was a lull in the bigger discussion and the voice of Nathaniel was heard telling a story.

"Tortoise went on a long journey to a distant clan. But before he went he told his people not to send for him unless something new under the sun happened. When he was gone, his mother died. The question was how to make him return to bury his mother. If they told him that his mother had died, he would say it was nothing new. So they told him that his father's palm tree had borne a fruit at the end of its leaf. When tortoise heard this, he said he must return home to see this great monstrosity. And so his bid to escape the burden of his mother's funeral was foiled."

There was a long and embarrassed silence when Nathaniel finished his story. It was clear that he had not meant it for more than a few ears around him. But he had suddenly found himself talking to the whole room. And he was not the man to stop in midstory.

Again Obi slept all night and woke up in the morning with a feeling of guilt. But it was not as poignant as yesterday's. And it very soon vanished altogether, leaving a queer feeling of calm. Death was a very odd thing, he thought. His mother was not three days dead and yet she was already so distant. When he tried last night to picture her he found the picture a little blurred at the edges.

"Poor mother!" he said, trying by manipulation to produce the right emotion. But it was no use. The dominant feeling was of peace.

He had a large and unseemly appetite when breakfast came, but he deliberately refused to eat more than a very little. At eleven, however, he could not help drinking a little *garri* soaked in cold water with sugar. As he drank it with a spoon he caught himself humming a dance tune.

"Terrible!" he said.

Then he remembered the story of King David, who refused food when his beloved son was sick, but washed and ate when he died. He, too, must have felt this kind of peace. The peace that passeth all understanding.

CHAPTER NINETEEN

WHEN THE PERIOD OF GUILT WAS OVER OBI FELT LIKE metal that has passed through fire. Or, as he himself put it in one of his spasmodic entries in his diary: "I wonder why I am feeling like a brand-new snake just emerged from its slough." The picture of his poor mother returning from the stream, her washing undone and her palm bleeding where his rusty blade had cut into it, vanished. Or rather it took a secondary place. He now remembered her as the woman who got things done.

His father, although uncompromising in conflicts between church and clan, was not really a man of action but of thought. It was true he sometimes took precipitous and violent decisions, but such occasions were rare. When faced with a problem under normal circumstances, he was apt to weigh it and measure it and look it up and down, postponing action. He relied heavily on his wife at such moments. He always said in jest that it all started on their wedding day. And he would tell how she had cut the cake first.

When the missionaries brought their own kind of marriage, they also brought the wedding cake. But it was soon adapted to suit the people's sense of drama. The bride and the groom were given a knife each. The master of ceremonies counted "One, two, three, go!" And the first to cut through the cake was the senior partner. On Isaac's wedding day his wife had cut the cake first.

But the story that Obi came to cherish even more was that of the sacred he-goat. In his second year of marriage his father was catechist in a place called Aninta. One of the great gods of Aninta was Udo, who had a he-goat that was dedicated to him. This goat became a menace at the mission. Apart from resting and leaving droppings in the church, it destroyed the catechist's yam and maize crops. Mr. Okonkwo complained a number of times to the priest of Udo, but the priest (no doubt a humorous old man) said that Udo's he-goat was free to go where it pleased and do what it pleased. If it chose to rest in Okonkwo's shrine, it probably showed that their two gods were pals. And there the matter would have stood had not the he-goat one day entered Mrs. Okonkwo's kitchen and eaten up the yam she was preparing to cook—and that at a season when yam was as precious as elephant tusks. She took a sharp matchet and hewed off the beast's head. There were angry threats from village elders. The women for a time refused to buy from her or sell to her in the market. But so successful had been the emasculation of the clan by the white man's religion and government that the matter soon died down. Fifteen years before this incident the men of Aninta had gone to war with their neighbors and reduced them to submission. Then the white man's government had stepped in and ordered the surrender of all firearms in Aninta. When they had all been collected, they were publicly broken by soldiers. There is an age grade in Aninta today called the Age Group of the Breaking of the Guns. They are the children born in that year.

These thoughts gave Obi a queer kind of pleasure. They seemed to release his spirit. He no longer felt guilt. He, too, had died. Beyond death there are no ideals and no humbug, only reality. The impatient idealist says: "Give me a place to stand and I shall move the earth." But such a place does not exist. We all have to stand on the earth itself and go with her at her pace. The most horrible sight in the world cannot put out the eye. The death of a mother is not like a palm tree bearing fruit at the end of its leaf, no matter how much we want to make it so. And that is not the only illusion we have. . . .

It was again the season for scholarships. There was so much work now that Obi had to take some files home every day. He was just settling down to work when a new model Chevrolet pulled up outside. He saw it quite clearly from his writing desk. Who could it be? It looked like one of those prosperous Lagos businessmen. Whom could he want? All the other occupants of the flat were unimportant Europeans on the lower rungs of the civil service.

The man knocked on Obi's door, and Obi jumped up to open it for him. He probably wanted to ask him the way to somewhere else. Nonresidents of Ikoyi always got lost among its identical flats.

"Good afternoon," he said.

"Good afternoon. Are you Mr. Okonkwo?"

Obi said yes. The man came in and introduced himself. He wore a very expensive *agbada*.

"Please have a seat."

"Thank you." He brought out a little towel from somewhere in the folds of his flowing gown and mopped his face. "I don't want to waste your time," he said, mopping one forearm and then the other under the wide sleeves of his *agbada*. "My son is going to England in September. I want him to get scholarship. If you can do it for me here is fifty pounds." He brought out a wad of notes from the front pocket of his *agbada*.

Obi told him it was not possible. "In the first place I don't give scholarships. All I do is go through the applications and recommend those who satisfy the requirements to the Scholarship Board."

"That's all I want," said the man. "Just recommend him."

"But the Board may not select him."

"Don't worry about that. Just do your own . . ."

Obi was silent. He remembered the boy's name. He was already on the short list, "Why don't you pay for him? You have money. The scholarship is for poor people."

The man laughed. "No man has money in this world." He rose to his feet, placed the wad of notes on the occasional table before Obi. "This is just small kola," he said. "We will make good friends. Don't forget the name. We will see again. Do you ever go to the club? I have never seen you before."

"I'm not a member."

"You must join," he said. "Bye-bye."

The wad of notes lay where he had placed it for the rest of the day and all night. Obi placed a newspaper over it and secured the door. "This is terrible!" he muttered. "Terrible!" he said aloud. He woke up with a start in the middle of the night and he did not go to sleep again for a long time afterwards.

"You dance very well," he whispered as she pressed herself against him, breathing very fast and hard. He put her arms round his neck and brought her lips within a centimeter of his. They no longer paid any attention to the beat of the high-life. Obi steered her towards his bedroom. She made a halfhearted show of resisting, then followed.

Obviously she was not an innocent schoolgirl. She knew her job. She was on the short list already, anyway. All the same, it was a great letdown. No point in pretending that it wasn't. One should at least be honest. He took her back to Yaba in his car. On his return journey he called on Christopher to tell him about it so that perhaps they might laugh it off. But he left again without having told the story. Some other day, perhaps.

Others came. People would say that Mr. So-and-so was a gentleman. He would take money, but he would do his stuff, which was a big advertisement, and others would follow. But Obi stoutly refused to countenance anyone who did not possess the minimum educational and other requirements. On that he was unshakeable.

In due course he paid off his bank overdraft and his debt to the Hon. Sam Okoli, M.H.R. The worst was now over, and Obi ought to have felt happier. But he didn't.

Then one day someone brought twenty pounds. As the man left, Obi realized that he could stand it no more. People say that one gets used to these things, but he had not found it like that at all. Every incident had been a hundred times worse than the one before it. The money lay on the table. He would have preferred not to look in its direction, but he seemed to have no choice. He just sat looking at it, paralyzed by his thoughts.

There was a knock at the door. He sprang to his feet, grabbed the money, and ran towards his bedroom. A second knock caught him almost at the door of the bedroom and transfixed him there. Then he saw on the floor for the first time the hat which his visitor had forgotten, and he breathed a sigh of relief. He thrust the money into his pocket and went to the door and opened it. Two people entered—one was his recent visitor, the other a complete stranger.

"Are you Mr. Okonkwo?" asked the stranger. Obi said yes in a voice he could hardly have recognized. The room began to swim round and round. The stranger was saying something, but it sounded distant—as things sound to a man in a fever. He then searched Obi and found the marked notes. He began to say some more things, invoking the name of the Queen, like a District Officer in the bush reading the Riot Act to an uncomprehending and delirious mob. Meanwhile the other man used the telephone outside Obi's door to summon a police van.

Everybody wondered why. The learned judge, as we have seen, could not comprehend how an educated young man and so on and so forth. The British Council man, even the men of Umuofia, did not know. And we must presume that, in spite of his certitude, Mr. Green did not know either.

Uniquely and richly African:

Chinua Achebe

recreates with energy
and authenticity
major issues and daily life
in Africa.